MASTERING MAYHEM

FIRE WITCHES OF SALEM
BOOK SIX

CARRIE PULKINEN

Mastering Mayhem

ISBN: 978-1-957253-24-4

CHAPTER I

MAYHEM

My soul, my life, my reason for *being* lay limp in my arms, her stillness carving a crater in my chest and hollowing my stomach until nothing but blind rage remained inside me.

Rage I could not contain.

"Is she...?" A tear slid down Ash's cheek as I moved Ember from my lap to hers.

"She's alive. Barely." I rose to my feet, my eyes heating, my irises undulating as the fury built. "I wouldn't be here otherwise."

"Mile—" She choked on a sob and rested the back of her fingers on her sister's forehead. "Give me my satchel."

Ember was in expert hands with Ash and the others, which allowed me to focus on the Formorian dangling from my brother's clutches...the reason my beloved barely clung to a frayed thread of existence.

"You will return her life force to her body, *Donal*." I spoke the culpable creature's name with such force, he flinched.

The vile beast kicked, flailing his arms and legs. My brother squeezed his throat harder, yet Donal did not obey. He was a son of Balor, after all. When his race ran rampant, his power matched my own. Even using his name, he was difficult to control.

My fury boiled over, hellfire heating every inch of my skin and threatening to erupt.

"She's not breathing." Ash laid Ember on the floor and blew into her mouth, making her chest rise and fall. "How is she alive if she's not breathing?" Her voice took on an edge of shrillness as she placed her hands over Ember's heart and repeatedly compressed her chest.

"Alive, alive for the time." Donal grasped Chaos's arm with both hands. "Let me go, and I'll send her home."

My brother lowered him to the floor but kept a firm grip on the beast's throat. "You will not disappear, Donal. You will do exactly as we say."

"You want me to send her home, yes?" His voice was thin, his breath barely escaping his compressed throat.

"Yes," Chaos growled.

"Release me, and it's done." Donal patted his hand. "Let go, big guy, and I'll send her on high."

"No! He's a trickster." I grabbed the creature's arm, wrenching it behind his back as my brother released him. "You will not send her *on high*, Donal. You will return her life force to her body."

He strained, the grinding of his teeth audible as he fought my command. "We should be equals. Tell me your name since I've done the same."

"You didn't tell us anything." I twisted his arm up his back, wrenching it harder. "And we will never be equals, you sniveling, rhyming imp. Now, return my witch's life force."

He hissed through his teeth. "Father needs it."

"Ember needs it." Grabbing the back of his neck, I swung him toward my witch and shoved him to his knees. "Give it back to her, Donal."

"Do it, Donal," Chaos said.

Ash stood, allowing Miles to continue breathing for Ember, sparks gathering on her fingertips as she loomed over the vile beast. "Donal, you better do it right now before I beat you to a pulp and burn you beyond recognition."

He groaned, his body tensing as he ground out, "No."

A fireball formed in Ash's hand, and she hurled it at his chest, setting his shirt ablaze. The Formorian squealed and writhed in my grasp, but I held him firmly, forcing him to feel Ash's wrath.

"If you want her to stop, you will do as we say." I twisted his arm again, and his shoulder dislodged from its socket with a *pop*.

"Enough." Chaos placed a hand on Ash's shoulder.

"Don't you dare try to calm me down." She shrugged him off and grabbed a handful of Donal's hair, angling his head upward and forcing him to look at her. "Do. It. Now."

Smoke rose from her fist, the stench of burning hair joining the reek of charred flesh.

"Okay, okay! Make the burning stop!" Tears streamed down his face, rolling around his snotty pig snout before dripping onto the floor.

Ash called her fire back and released his hair. The Formorian's shirt had turned to ash, but his burns healed in seconds. He blew out a hard breath, his body slumping into my grasp.

"My arm hurts. Let me go, and I'll do the work."

My eyes narrowed, and I cut my gaze toward Chaos and Ash. They nodded, and Ash moved to my right, the three of us flanking the creature while Miles poured a potion into Ember's mouth.

"Do not disappear, Donal." I loosened my grip, allowing him to lean toward Ember.

"My arm, please."

I let go, and he gripped his dislocated shoulder,

forcing it back into place before resting both hands on the floor and crawling toward my witch. He paused and whispered something in the Formorian tongue. Before I could react, he grabbed a handful of ashes, flinging them into our faces and scrambling away.

I blinked against the grit in my eyes and gave chase. Our command that he not disappear remained, but the order to return Ember's life force had never taken hold. He threw clothing racks and toppled display cases as he darted for the storage room door.

I leaped over the obstacles, plowing toward him. My new ostrich boots—the only items of clothing remaining on my demon form—caught on a tangle of western shirts, making me stumble.

I kicked off the offending shoes, and my hooves clomped on the linoleum as I lunged for the door, catching it before it could close. "Donal, you sorry excuse for a lifeform, return Ember's energy imme- diately."

"Never will I ever. Father needs it." He darted around a corner as Chaos entered the room.

My brother gripped my shoulder. "Balor is here."

"Whatever gave you that idea?" I stormed forward, stopping short of the corner as a wave of dizziness washed over me. My fingers and nose tingled, purple smoke escaping the undersides of my talons.

Chaos's brow slammed down, his irises rippling. "We're losing her...and you."

"Thank you for pointing out the obvious." I pressed forward, though it felt like I was moving through a tarpit. My muscles screamed, the fabric of my being shredding from the inside out as the Underworld called me home.

"Grab him," Ash shouted from behind me. "I know an extraction spell. We'll force Ember's energy from his body."

One foot in front of the other, I rounded the corner, the force of each step ricocheting through my body, threatening to shatter my bones the moment my hoof hit the floor.

Donal sat on his knees, his hands on the floor, straddling a lump of rotting flesh. "This is a strong one, Father."

He opened his mouth, and glittering gold energy—the essence of Ember's being—crossed his lips, spiraling into the creature beneath him.

The pain in my body ceased, the instinct to save the woman I loved taking complete control and rendering me numb to everything except my purpose. I lunged for Donal, hauling him up by his neck and clutching his throat.

"Balor, Balor, I have valor," he squeaked. "Look what I brought you, Father."

"Give it to me," the lump on the floor wheezed. "Or you're worth less than a sneeze."

"I've had enough of your rhyming, imbecile." I

squeezed his neck, my talons digging into his skin and making him bleed. "Last chance. Return Ember's life force."

"Hold him still." Ash dumped a jar of herbs onto the floor.

"Never." He opened his mouth, and Ember's energy shot toward Balor.

My stomach lurched. I tightened my grip, jerking my hand and snapping his neck. The wretched bastard screamed, but my witch's energy continued to flow. Ash lit the herbs ablaze and began reciting an incantation, but I barely heard her words. Purple smoke rose from my skin. My body, once solid, wavered, my corporeal form trying to skate away as Ember's hold on the thread of life slipped.

I could wait no longer.

With the Formorian still dangling from my grasp, I plunged my talons into his chest. His ribs cracked and splintered as I reached for his heart.

"Mayhem, no!" Ash's voice echoed somewhere in the distance.

Twisting and ripping, I dislodged the organ from his veins, yanking it out and tossing Donal's corpse onto the floor.

The heart beat three times in my hand before crumbling to dust along with his body.

Ember's energy rose from the pile, gathering into a ball of light before drifting toward the ceiling. A pricking sensation formed on my skin, and more purple smoke—my essence—seeped from my pores.

I looked at my brother and then at Ash. "I'm fading."

"No shit." Her brown furrowed. "I had an extraction spell ready, but this..." She gestured to the beautiful ball of sparkling light. "I need to mix a containment spell before she crosses over."

A sob rolled up from my chest, but I caught it in my throat and reached a hand into the light. My witch's essence, her energy, her life danced across my waning skin, making my stomach clench. Ember had a kind, pure soul. She would not be damned to my realm.

Which meant I would never see her again.

I squared my gaze on Ash. "You have to save her."

"And you have to quit trying to solve every situation with violence." She swiped a mixture of herbs around the lip of a small container. "Light of life, avoiding strife. Don't go far; enter this jar. As I will it, so mote it be."

The light shimmered. It spread across the ceiling, casting the room in shades of gold and silver as if both the sun and the moon were working together to illuminate the mess I had made.

"No. It's mine." Balor blew out a breath and inhaled deeply. Ember's energy shimmied, drifting toward the king of the Formorians.

"Ash..." My legs weakened. The low vibration of

the Underworld called me home, but I fought it. Home was not in the pits of Hell. Not anymore. Home was no longer a place…it was a person.

Home was Ember.

Ash recited the spell again. Still, Ember's light flowed toward Balor.

No. No, this was not happening. I would not return to Hell. I refused to let Ember die.

Dropping to my knees, I shoved my talons into Balor's chest. His bones had not hardened, so my claws passed through easily, even in my weakened state. I fisted my hand where his heart should have been, but his insides were nothing but gelatinous sludge.

How could I vanquish the vile beast if he had no heart?

He let out a pained mewl as I swirled my hand inside his chest, stirring his insides like soup. I hoped it was the most excruciating agony he had ever felt.

Ember's light stilled. Then, it vibrated. It dimmed and pulsed, shimmying between Balor and Ash.

"Balor, I demand you release her." I plunged my talons upward, toward his throat, the tips protruding from the base of his neck. His eyes bulged, and he wheezed.

Ash spoke the incantation a third time. Ember's light flashed twice and soared toward the jar Ash held.

It flowed into the container, sparkling like a thousand fireflies danced within the glass.

"Come on. Chaos will watch him." She closed the jar and grasped my arm, tugging me away from the beast. "We need to save Ember."

I followed her into the store. Miles held Ember's head in his lap. When he looked up, a tear slid down his cheek. "I don't know what else to do," he said.

"She's not gone yet." Shade adjusted his position, wincing and pressing a hand to his injured stomach. "But, dude, you're smoking."

I dropped to the floor and pulled my witch into my lap, brushing the matted hair from her forehead. Ash lowered to her knees and opened the jar, holding it toward Ember's face. As her light rose from the container, my smoke swirled around it, creating a protective cocoon.

I could feel her in my soul, lighting the darkness inside me, making me whole.

"Let it go," Ash said. "Her energy can't return while you're holding it hostage."

"I can't." I tried. I tried to call my smoke into my corporeal form, but this body was merely a vessel about to sink. My soul refused to let her go.

Ash grabbed my wrist. "You have to, or she'll die."

More smoke rose from my skin, my body becoming translucent as Ember slipped further and further into the ether. "Take her. Save her."

Ash pulled Ember into her lap, and I crawled away, my legs too weak to carry me. As I moved, my smoke followed, still attached to my semi-solid form. A trail extended to Ember's light, the once-invisible tether holding her tightly in this realm.

Ash looked at me, tilting her head and silently reminding me I had to let her go to save her.

I backed away, dragging myself across the floor and willing the Underworld to let me remain. My soul released her, the agony that followed unbearable. A rift opened above me. My essence flowed toward it.

"Come on, Em. Take it back." Ash fanned the light toward her sister's face.

I could not fight the pull. My arms dissipated into smoke and flowed into the rift. My legs followed, the disintegration inching its way toward my torso until darkness closed in around me.

CHAPTER 2
EMBER

I wanted the pain to stop. My entire body ached and burned. The sensation of a million electrified needles jabbing into my nerves and joints made me both swelter and shiver...convulse...in agony.

My pain tolerance had always been higher than most. My level four could be another person's nine, so I normally considered the discomfort scale from one to ten at the doctor's office useless.

Not this time. No, not now.

On a scale of one to ten, my *discomfort* was a thirty-plus.

I'd felt fine a minute ago. At least, I'd thought I did. Honestly, I couldn't remember much after Mayhem put on the ridiculously expensive clothes and my credit card got rejected.

If you can't pay, you have to stay.

How did I end up on the floor? Did George…?

And why did my nose feel like I'd inhaled a tablespoon of crushed red pepper?

I tried to blow a puff of air through my nostrils, but my body disobeyed the command from my foggy brain and did the opposite instead. I snorted. Then I coughed, wheezing in more and more pepper until my throat burned and my lungs expanded and contracted as if I were hyperventilating.

"Oh, thank the goddess." That was Ash's voice, but either my eyes wouldn't open or I'd gone blind from the pain.

"Come on, Em," she said in a motherly tone. "Breathe it all in."

"Pain…" I rasped.

"I know it hurts, but you have to." A sob choked off her last words. "Mayhem needs you."

Mayhem…

I sucked in another breath. Razorblades sliced into my lungs. My heart did this weird *thud…thud-thud-thud* thing. Mayhem needed me. George… He'd trapped my demon with the ouroboros bracelet.

Nobody trapped *my demon.*

Another breath raked through my lungs, and I licked my chapped lips. Bits of skin clung to my tongue, making my stomach turn. A warm cloth pressed against my eyes, Ash's gentle hand wiping away the crust holding them closed.

One opened halfway, the inner corner still matted with gunk. My vision swam. Miles held the cloth, not my sister. He swiped my right eye again, and it opened fully.

Light pierced my pupil like a white-hot needle, and I fought the urge to squeeze my lid shut and sleep. Mayhem needed me. I couldn't let him down.

"Another breath, Em. You have to take it all." Ash held a jar beneath my nose. What spicy potion had she mixed up to bring me into consciousness? Whatever it was, I hoped to never experience it again.

I might as well have sucked a ghost pepper through each nostril, and oh, man... Hot in was hot out. I was not looking forward to my first trip to the bathroom.

Miles wiped my left eye, and I pried it open.

"There she is." He smiled, but he couldn't mask the concern carving crevasses into his forehead.

I blinked the fogginess from my vision as Ash returned the jar to her bag. "Why does it feel like someone hit me with a Hummer, backed over me, and plowed into me again?"

Ash's eyes glistened. "Because you almost died."

"I can tell." I tried to sit up, but my muscles screamed. The sigil on my arm felt raw...like someone had attempted to rip the magical ink from my skin. "Mayhem?"

Ash gestured with her head, and I followed her gaze to find my demon lying on the floor, unconscious. "What...?"

"He was almost sucked into the Underworld." Shade rose to his feet, wincing and clutching his stomach. "We almost lost you both."

"Is he okay?" I pushed to sitting, and the world turned on its side. My stomach lurched. My head pounded. My breakfast made a reappearance on the floor.

All I'd eaten was a protein bar, thankfully, but the bitter taste of stomach acid made me heave again.

"Here." Ash handed me a bottle of water.

I swished and spit before taking three huge gulps. Big mistake. It felt like forcing avocado pits through a cocktail straw. "What happened? Why do I hurt so much?"

Ash wiped the corner of my mouth with a cloth. "George... His real name is Donal. He sucked out your life force and was trying to feed it to his father."

"Huh?" My lids fluttered, my foggy brain unable to process her words. "His father?"

"Donal is a Formorian. A son of Balor." Shade toed Mayhem with his boot, and my demon rolled onto his back, his chest rising and falling with his slow, steady breaths.

He would be okay. That much I could comprehend, but my face must've been contorted in confusion because Ash patted my knee, her eyes holding so much sympathy, I nearly choked.

"The fae eradicated the species eons ago," she said, "but somehow Donal escaped and brought Balor with him to our realm."

I sighed, closing my eyes and leaning against the wall. "And he opened a store?" Sure, the fog in my brain was jumbling my thoughts, but I couldn't have made sense of her words if I were operating at full capacity. "Why would he open a store?"

"Look. He's been feeding off his customers." She shook my shoulder, so I opened my eyes and followed her gesture to the adjacent wall. At least a dozen mummified bodies lined the space, their emaciated arms chained above their heads.

Holy Hecate. I wanted to feel bad for the people. I really did, but the pain in my muscles and the haze in my brain made it impossible to think about anything else.

Mayhem groaned and rolled to his side, facing us. His demon form, in all its glorious nakedness, didn't stir a single hormone inside me. I didn't even check out his junk.

His lids flew open, his eyes locking on me, his body moving half a second later.

"Ember!" He shot to his feet—erm, hooves—and clomped toward me before dropping to his knees and pulling me into his arms. "Thank Lucifer, you're alive."

My skin felt like road rash, his hands like sandpaper against it. "Ow."

"What's wrong?" He held my shoulders, pushing me back so he could look into my eyes. "What hurts?"

"Everything." My laugh turned into a sob. *Every-friggin-thing.*

He snapped his head toward Ash. "Did you return all of her light?"

She took the empty jar from her bag and held it toward him. "All of it."

A growl rumbled in his chest, and his grip tightened on my arms.

"Ow," I said again.

"I'm sorry." He released me, letting me slump against the wall before turning to Ash. "That wasn't all of it. Balor..."

"Crappity crap. You're right." Ash stood and slung her bag over her shoulder. "Donal had already given some of her life force to Balor when you vanquished him. Come on." She grabbed my arm, attempting to haul me to my feet, but my legs were too weak to hold me.

Mayhem scooped me into a cradle carry, my skin, my muscles, my joints protesting as he rose to his hooves. I didn't dare complain. If this Balor dude had a piece of me, I would wrench it from his clutches and rip his head from his body.

Just as soon as my own body recovered from whatever the hell happened to me.

We followed Ash into the back of the building where Chaos loomed over a rotted mass of *something*. He crossed his arms, keeping a wide stance, a look of disgust curling his lip. "Balor, you will return her life force."

My gaze snapped to the mound of flesh, my brain finally processing the shape. Balor, King of the Formorians, lay partially formed on the floor. His skin held an ashy-green pallor, his face almost skeletal as he reached an arm toward me.

"Sssshe's mine..." he hissed, and a tiny flame ignited on his fingertip.

Witch fire. *My* fire.

"Oh, hell no. That's mine." I wiggled in Mayhem's arms, and he lowered my feet to the floor, keeping a firm grip on my shoulders so I didn't topple over.

Balor inched toward me, his blob of a body moving like a slug. "Give it to me, and I'll set you free."

"I'm already free, you wannabe Jabba the Hutt." If I had my sword—and if my legs would carry me—I'd lob off his head and make his species extinct for good. Sadly, in my current condition, I was about as useful as wet toilet paper. Single ply.

"Ash, I need an extraction spell." I made a grabby motion toward her. No way in hell could I cast it alone.

"On it, but you're not helping." Before I could protest, she lit some herbs on fire and took Miles's hand.

They recited the incantation together, and Balor's semi-gelatinous form bubbled, his thin skin turning transparent as my energy fought his hold. He strained, his expression looking like he was both constipated and trying not to puke at the same time. I knew the feeling.

Well, not the constipation part. But if my stomach didn't stop lurching every time I twitched, it—along with all my innards—might end up on the floor.

"Nooo… Make it stop," Balor wailed.

Mayhem's growl rumbled through my body, setting my nerves off on a tangent. "How did you escape Hell?"

"Donal did. Please stooooop." My light, a shimmering gold, gathered beneath the surface of his skin.

"How long have you been in this realm?" Ash asked. "Answer us and we'll make the pain stop."

"Months. Months! Rifts in the veil. Donal is smart. Lots of heart."

My stomach heaved. A drumline pounded out a sickening rhythm in my head while Balor's agonizing wails jabbed daggers into my ears. Goosebumps pricked my skin, the fever making me shiver and sweat, and I leaned into Mayhem, willing myself to stay upright. "Let's put him out of his misery."

Ash and Miles recited the incantation two more times in succession. Balor's mouth opened, his jaw unhinging like Imhotep from *The Mummy*, as my light poured from his throat. It shot toward me and blasted up my nostrils, burning like a mixture of Carolina Reaper and ghost pepper oils.

Damn, I was a spicy witch.

I heaved in three breaths, four, five, until the burning stopped and the drumline ceased their incessant song. My eyes and mouth watered, the cracks in my lips healing and plumping as my life force surged through my body. The strength returning to my muscles, I stepped out of Mayhem's arms and leered at the heap of wasted flesh on the floor.

"There's a reason your kind went extinct." I reached back for my sword, but my hand met only air. "Please tell me someone brought my weapons inside."

Ash shook her head. Balor wheezed, attempting to form words, but without my energy, he'd turned into a slimy blob of yuck...yuckier than he was before.

"His heart hasn't fully formed." Mayhem held up a taloned hand. "I tried to wrench it from his chest, but his entrails are gelatinous."

"That's fine. He has a head I can lob off."

"Here." Shade offered me a twelve-inch dagger. "It's the sharpest one I've got."

I accepted the blade, holding the leather-wrapped handle and testing its weight. "Nice."

Our Jabba wannabe inched away like the slug he was, so I grabbed a handful of his sparse hair, angling his head up and exposing the rolls of his fatty neck.

My grip tightened on the handle, and I was about to jab the blade into his throat when a sense of peace washed over me. My brain had the audacity to search for a non-violent solution to allow Balor to remain in existence.

I narrowed my eyes, cutting my gaze toward my demon. "Mayhem!"

"Sorry." He drew his shoulders upward and tilted his head down like a scolded puppy, which was kind of cute considering he stood there in all his princely demonic gloriousness.

His magic dissipated from my psyche, and I looked at Ash. "Is there any reason I shouldn't vanquish this asshat right now, and does anyone want to help me?"

"Go for it," she said. "He's all yours."

I jabbed the blade into his neck. The razor edges passed through his flesh as if he were made of margarine, severing his head with one clean stroke. My fingers still clutching Balor's hair, I lifted my prize triumphantly.

"Mmm..." Mayhem's growl sounded more like a purr. "You are a warrior goddess."

Did I mention he was naked? My gaze locked on

his massive package, which no longer hung freely in the breeze. His soldier stood at attention, and he licked his lips, his irises rippling like they did when he wanted to devour me.

"You might want to find some clothes." I waved the dagger in the direction of his junk and dropped Balor's head. It rolled, stopping face-up and blinking at me. "Holy shit. He's not dead."

"The only way to vanquish a Formorian is to destroy his heart." Mayhem morphed into his human form, and his soldier finally stood at ease...ish. It was getting there, anyway. "And he has no heart to destroy."

I forced my gaze to his eyes. "So, what then? Are we just going to leave him here, headless?"

"That would be cruel," Miles said.

"And dangerous." Ash set her satchel on the floor and examined the contents. "If humans come in and find him, he could still drain their energy. We can't take that chance."

"No, we can't." I spotted a shelf filled with packs of men's undies, so I grabbed one and tossed it to Mayhem. "Put those on. It's hard to focus with...all that."

He chuckled and opened the pouch, pulling out a pair of dark gray boxer-briefs. With his package wrapped, I turned my attention to my sister.

"We need a spell to solidify his heart." She lined up

three herb bottles on the floor. "If we can force it to form, then we can destroy it."

"We could do that." I eyed the disgusting creature. "But why waste our vim?"

My palm tingled, a fireball igniting on my skin. I tipped my hand, dropping the flames onto Balor's severed head. His hair lit up like a bonfire, and a gurgling sound emanated from his neck as his chest expanded and contracted.

"That hurts, doesn't it?" I picked him up by the ear and dropped his head onto his body. "You picked on the wrong witch."

I shot flames from both hands, setting his entire body ablaze. "You guys might want to step outside the room. It's about to get hot in here."

"It already is." Shade squinted, lifting a hand to shield his face from the flames as he and Miles returned to the front of the store.

"I guess your way works." Ash's expression scrunched, and she placed the bottles in her bag before rising to her feet and adding to my flames. "Incinerate his entire body, and the molecules that would make up his heart burn too."

"Exactly. How about a little hellfire, guys?" I shot another flame and watched the bastard burn.

His form began to melt in our witch flames, and when Mayhem and Chaos shot streams of hellfire into the fray, it crumbled. The fire raged, consuming every piece of the Formorian until nothing but a pile of opaque crystals remained.

"Good riddance." I called my fire back and brushed my palms together as if I could dust off this entire ordeal.

"It needs to be hotter." Mayhem grasped my elbow. "Until he turns to ash, he still exists on this plane."

As if to prove his point, the crystals of Balor vibrated, bouncing off each other, sliding this way and that across the floor until several melded together. Another handful stuck into a clump, bubbling and making a sickening, goopy sound as they formed into a glassy eyeball. It rolled, squaring its gaze—if it could even see—on me.

"You have got to be kidding me." I stomped the eye, squishing it beneath my boot heel.

"Again." Mayhem shot a stream of white-hot hell-fire at the remains.

"Ash!" Miles shouted from the next room. "Shade's hemorrhaging. I need your help."

"Gods, I miss Patrice. Can you...?" she asked.

"We've got this. Go." I added my flames to Mayhem's.

"Assist your witch," Mayhem said to Chaos. "Ember and I will handle the beast. This is personal."

"Damn right, it is." I sent another wave of heat into the bonfire of Balor as they rushed out to save Shade.

My flames, bright orange with a base of blue, swirled and spun through Mayhem's white ones. He cut his gaze to me, one corner of his mouth lifting in a grin as he took a deep breath and added to the inferno.

His fire morphed from white to blue to indigo, the tips turning a vibrant purple as it flickered and consumed. The combination of colors shifted and blended, pirouetting and swaying together in a mesmerizing dance of magic.

"It's beautiful, isn't it? The way our colors blend." He slid an arm around my waist. "We are good together."

"When we're not trying to kill each other, yeah."

He dropped his hand to his side, stepping away from me and focusing on the flames.

It took a minute. Okay, more like ten, but finally the crystals smoked, smoldered, and turned into ashes. I called back my flames and heaved a breath. That was enough physical exertion for one day. *Whew*.

"Are your boots fireproof?" he asked.

"Everything I wear is. Why?"

"Lift your foot."

"Why?" I raised a knee, and he sighed.

"The other one." He grabbed my pants at the ankle and raised the sole of my boot toward him. "Even this small amount of the Formorian's eye on your shoe is enough for him to reform." He lit the tip of his finger ablaze. "Unless you want to take him to New York?"

"Fire away." If I ever saw one of these revolting creatures again, it would be way too soon.

With my boot cleansed in flames, I curled my lip at what was left of our captors and followed Mayhem to the front of the store. Shade lay on the floor, a washcloth over his eyes, his stomach exposed.

My heart sank. "Is he okay?"

"He'll be fine." Ash swiped a magical salve across the stitches. "This will speed the healing, but you'll have a massive scar."

"That's okay." Shade pulled the cloth from his eyes. "Chicks dig scars."

Miles shot his gaze to the floor before rising to his feet, and I had to wonder if Shade had any clue about his feelings for him. It wasn't my place to ask, so I went shopping in what was left of the store.

Mayhem had torn through his new, ridiculously expensive clothes when he let his demon loose, so I grabbed him another pair of starched jeans and a black button-up. He dressed and put on his new boots while I grabbed myself a slinky little black number from the women's section. Since I couldn't take weapons into the auction house, I might as well dress the part of the trophy wife, right?

"We aren't going to pay, and we don't have to stay." I gave the cash register the middle finger and turned toward the door. "Let's roll."

Chaos helped Miles support Shade, and we all

finally left the building. Well, all of us except Mayhem. He stood in the doorway, his expression livid.

"Come on," I said.

He held up his arm, showing me the ouroboros on his wrist. "I can't."

I sighed, my posture deflating. "Well, shit."

CHAPTER 3
EMBER

"Hey, Ash. Bring your bag. We've got a problem." I stomped back into the store, silently swearing to the gods before narrowing my eyes at Mayhem. "I told you not to try on the bracelet."

"And I heeded your warning." He crossed his arms. "If you remember, you told me to change into my normal clothes. Donal put the ouroboros on me when I reached for them."

I clutched his forearm and rotated the bracelet on his wrist, making the snake shiver and chomp its tail harder. "I remember."

"Then why are you angry with me?"

Well, let's see. I'd almost died...had the life literally sucked out of me. He'd almost been vanquished because of it. Wasn't I allowed to be a little snippy?

If I wanted to dig in deep—which I didn't—I'd admit I wasn't angry. I'd tell him the truth: that I was scared to death of my feelings for him and that losing him—which was inevitable—would crush me, so I shut down at every mention of our goddess-forsaken *un*happily ever after.

I couldn't think about it, much less talk about it. Thankfully, Ash came in and got right to work, saving me from my thought spiral.

She set her bag on the counter and pulled out a bowl and six herb jars. "Did Donal tell you anything about the bracelet? I can mix the potion I use to neutralize the unsavory magical artifacts I find in the thrift shops, but I don't know if it will work on Formorian magic."

"He believed I was a witch when he put it on me," Mayhem said.

She pursed her lips. "That's not helpful."

I drummed my fingers on the countertop and grinned. "We could save our vim and chop off his instead. Got a knife?"

Mayhem rolled his eyes. "You are always a comedian, aren't you?"

"I try." Anything to deflect the thoughts, because he was right. It was beautiful, the way the colors of our fire blended. And our fire was deeply rooted in our souls, which meant our souls would blend beautifully if I gave them the chance.

Damn it. I was still thinking. I blamed the adrenaline still flooding my veins.

Ash mixed the herbs and poured six drops of lavender oil into the bowl. "The magic in the bracelet is strong enough to hold a demon prince. Neutralizing it won't be easy."

"Which is why we should just chop off his wrist." I clamped my mouth shut. *Really, Em?* The man only wanted to love me, but every time he broke down a layer of my heart wall, I slapped another glob of mortar on it and added more bricks.

I couldn't tell you what the hell was wrong with me, but it needed to stop. He only wanted to love me. My chest tightened and warmed at the thought. My stomach also looped, and a swarm of moths tried to take flight inside me, so there was that. I had hormones pinging off nerve cells and innards rising and sinking. I needed an hour in one of those sensory deprivation tanks to sort it all out.

"Sure," Ash said. "Let's chop off his wrist and have him bleed out before we make it to New York. Great plan." She stirred the potion, and it smoked, the clean scents of lavender and mint adding to the sickly sweet smell in the air.

"I wonder what spell he cast to neutralize the stench of death." I scanned the far wall, where the dozen-plus bodies sat chained. "Do you think they're all witches, or would human energy work to reform the disgusting king?"

"It doesn't matter what they were," Mayhem said. "They're dead now and not our concern."

"I feel bad for their families." I forced my gaze away. "They must be wondering where they are."

"And we must focus on the task at hand." He held up his magically shackled arm.

"He's right, Em." Ash shot a tiny flame into the potion, activating it. "A lot more people are going to die if we don't get the amulet, and I seriously don't want to be the one who kills them. Donal's body count has nothing to do with us."

Chaos stepped into the storefront. "Miles is tending to Shade in the van. He said we must hurry if he's to have enough time to set up his equipment and hack into the auction house's security system."

"Potion's ready." Ash returned the bottles to her bag and poured a pink powder into her palm before holding her free hand toward her demon. "We need all the help we can get. Come share your power with us."

He strode toward her and grasped her hand.

"I will share my power with you, Ember." Mayhem held his hand toward me.

I crossed my arms. "You're the one who's trapped, dummy. If your magic could break the bind, don't you think you'd have removed it by now?"

"Here. Take Chaos's hand." Ash poured half the powder into my palm, and I slipped my hand into his.

Mayhem's eyes narrowed, his nostrils flaring as his gaze locked on his brother. Was that jealousy I detected in his expression? And did the moths just multiply in my stomach?

Chaos gave me no time to ponder it. A surge of dark magic passed through my skin, filling me with demonic power that felt so different from Mayhem's. Chaos's low vibration—and lack of the pinpricking sensation I'd grown accustomed to with Mayhem—made me shudder.

I didn't like it. Not at all.

Ash sprinkled her half of the powdered potion onto the bracelet, and I did the same. Mayhem caught my gaze as I finished, the intensity in his eyes making me want to rip free from Chaos's hold and throw myself into *my* demon's arms.

Hecate have mercy; the emotion was strong.

"Ready?" Ash asked.

"Absolutely." The sooner I could get this *wrong* demon magic out of my system, the better.

I inhaled deeply, focusing my intent on the ouroboros. "Neutralize, dissolve, dismiss. This magic bind no longer exists."

We recited the incantation two times in unison, feeding off Chaos's power and using him as a channel as we opened ourselves to each other. My sister's high vibration mixed with her demon's low, tempering the sickening feeling in my stomach.

The snake writhed on Mayhem's wrist, eating more of its tail and growing tighter.

"It appears your spell is doing the opposite of what you intended," he said.

"We aren't finished." I touched three fingers to the bracelet, and Ash did the same. "Neutralize, dissolve, dismiss. This magic bind no longer exists. As we will it, so mote it be."

My head spun, and my stomach lurched, though I couldn't tell if it was from the wrongness of Chaos's power flowing through me or from the ouroboros fighting back. Another wave of demon magic crashed into me, and I squeezed my eyes shut, sending it down my arm and out my fingers, focusing everything I had on removing the damn bracelet.

"You're hurting her, brother," Mayhem said. "Release my witch."

"I'm fine." I strained, grinding my teeth until sharp pain shot from my jaw to my temple. I pushed one more surge of magic—mine, his, and Ash's—into the bracelet.

The snake hissed. Then it screamed. Its mouth opened, and I yanked the tail from its throat, hurling the offending little bastard across the room. Chaos let me go, and I stumbled forward, catching myself on Mayhem's chest.

My demon wrapped his arms around me, holding me as I sagged against him. I heaved in a breath, willing Chaos's magic to dissipate, and Mayhem stroked my hair, pressing a kiss to my aching temple as he tucked a lock behind my ear.

"I have you," he whispered. "You're safe now."

And goddess-dammit if I didn't *feel* safe wrapped in his embrace. Safe, secure, wanted, loved. I inhaled his warm campfire and cinnamon scent and allowed myself a moment—just a fleeting moment—before I pulled away and tucked another lock of hair behind my other ear. "I'm fine. This was our last side quest."

"Here's hoping." Ash handed me a cloth, and I wiped the remaining potion powder from my palm.

The building rumbled, the structure groaning against the weight of the roof. Ash looked at me wide-eyed before slinging her bag over her shoulder. "We need to go."

"Hold on." I scanned the room. The walls shimmered as if another layer of magic was dissolving around us. "How much glamour did Donal put on this place?"

"I'd rather not find out. Come on." My sister strode to the door, and Chaos followed her outside.

The walls and ceiling wavered as the magic dissipated. What was left of the clothing and accessories remained intact, which was a good thing. I doubted the auction house would allow good ol' Boyd "Big

Oil" from Texas into the building if his clothes dissolved.

"We should leave." Mayhem clutched my hand.

"I want to go shopping first." I tugged from his grasp and grabbed a shirt and a pair of stretchy cargo pants from a rack. "Size six. Perfect." I draped them over my arm along with the little black dress, and Mayhem arched a brow.

"He stole my life force. Comping an outfit or two is the least he can do." I jerked my head toward the exit, and he followed me outside.

My eyes watered in the blinding afternoon sun, and I turned my back against it, facing the store. The outside shimmered, shuddering and groaning, the façade wavering like heat coming off a blacktop. Starting from the rooftop, the magic melted away like candle wax, sliding down and revealing a decrepit barn where the store once stood.

"Holy mother of magic." I tilted my head, my brain refusing to accept the image my eyes clearly took in. "That's the most impressive cloak I've ever seen."

"The Formorians were known for their skill in deception." Mayhem rested a hand against the small of my back. "It's one of the reasons my kind worked with the fae to eradicate them. That and their mind-control power, which you witnessed today."

"When we get to New York, we'll make an anony-mous call to the police about the bodies. Eff you,

Formorian asshat." I gave what was left of "George's" store a one-fingered salute before turning on my heel and marching to the van.

Shade lay across Miles's lap in the middle seat, and Chaos and Ash sat squished into the half-seat in the way back.

"Is he going to be okay, or do we need to find a hospital?" I climbed into the driver's seat. The van was already running, the heater making it warm and toasty inside.

"I'll be fine." Shade struggled to sit up, but Miles rested a hand on his shoulder, gently holding him down.

"Ash used a salve she got from Patrice," Miles said. "It'll take an hour or so to finish, but he's already healing."

"Good. Everyone ready?"

"Yes, ma'am," Mayhem said in his fake Texas accent, and I suppressed a smile.

He gave new meaning to the expression *save a horse, ride a cowboy*. This demon was one cowboy I could ride all day long.

CHAPTER 4
MAYHEM

We arrived in New York, and Ember and I waited in the van while Chaos, Ash, and Miles stalked around the auction house, peering into the windows and taking photos of themselves in front of it to feign the roles of simple tourists.

The time they were away would have been perfect for a discussion about why Ember dismissed, with an ill-timed joke, my every mention of our bond. About why she'd pretended to be asleep when I had confessed my love to her.

Unfortunately, Shade remained in the van with us, recovering from his encounter with the Formorian's blade.

And oh, the noise...

New York City bustled with traffic—both vehicular

and pedestrian—the incessant sounds of engines revving, people shouting, and horns blaring grating on my nerves. It was all I could do to keep from sending them all into a fiery rage and letting them battle each other to the death.

"We've got a problem." Ash climbed into the van along with Chaos and Miles.

Ember pinched the bridge of her nose. "In addition to the eight hundred we're already dealing with?"

Miles shut the side door and slid past the others to reach the back of the van. "Ash found a ward on the building. A fresh one."

"Fantastic." Ember dropped her head back on the seat. "Fifty bucks says it's to keep out anyone with ill intent."

"Bingo." Ash rummaged through her bag. "I have the ingredients to get you through, but I'll need more room to work."

"And I need more room to move so I can think this through." Ember started the engine. "Anyway, I'm sure a black van sitting outside an auction house filled with a bajillion dollars' worth of artifacts isn't suspicious at all."

"I believe it's highly suspicious," I said. "Perhaps we should find a hotel room nearby."

She rolled her head toward me, not lifting it from the seat. "That was sarcasm. Did people not use it four hundred years ago?"

Most women did not, but I didn't dare say that aloud. Ember wasn't most women. She was unlike any I'd ever known.

Shade swiped his phone screen. "It's Friday. There's nothing affordable within twenty miles."

Ember shook her head, and I could almost hear the conflicting thoughts sparring in her mind, her morals insisting we pay for a room while her logical mind argued this quest required us to work in the gray.

"I believe this is one of your 'absolutely necessary' situations," I said. "Perhaps a little mind magic would take away the burden of your maxed-out credit card."

"He's right, Em." Ash leaned forward in her seat. "The closer we stay, the better. It would suck to get stuck in traffic and miss the whole thing."

"All right. Fine." She tugged on the gearshift, putting it into drive. "Where's the closest one with immediate availability?"

"Two blocks east," Miles said as he clicked the keys on the computer. "The Royal Dutch Hotel."

"I'd like to say this is the last time you can use this dark power, but I'm not an idiot." She pulled into the moving traffic, and the car behind her skidded, the wheels screeching as the horn blasted and the driver gave us the middle finger.

"When this is all over, though... No more." She ignored the man's gesture and drove into a parking garage, taking a small ticket from a machine before an orange apparatus lifted, granting us access. We spiraled upward, the low ceiling and dimly lit concrete corridor making me claustrophobic. Finally, she pulled into a spot and turned off the engine before sliding out of her seat and slamming the door.

"I don't like leaving all this equipment unattended," Miles said.

"We'll set up a ward." Ash opened the side door and climbed out of the van.

I joined Ember at the back of the vehicle, watching as she paced a short distance. She was tense, her jaw working from side to side as her shoulders tightened and drifted toward her ears. How I longed to rub the tension from her muscles like I had done a few days ago. Or was it yesterday? Time was meaningless to an immortal.

The moment the thought entered my mind, my chest pinched, an agonizing ache spreading through my body. Ember was mortal. Even if I found a way to stay in this realm, I would have to watch her grow old and die. For a moment, I forgot to breathe.

I couldn't bear it. I refused to think about it.

"Are you okay?" She caught my gaze. "You look like you want to punch something. That, or you ate a bad burrito and need to find the closest restroom."

I straightened, regaining my composure. "I'm fine. My bowels are also fine."

"Good," she said as the others joined us outside

the van. "Ash, Chaos, head to the front desk and get us one room. Just one, okay? Don't get greedy."

Her sister gave a mock salute.

"The rest of us will wait in the lobby." She looked from me to Miles and Shade. "Be as inconspicuous as possible. Don't do anything stupid."

"Got it," Shade said, and Miles nodded his understanding.

I arched a brow. "Anything for you, my feisty fire witch."

A ghost of a smile crossed her lips before she cleared her throat. "Let's go."

"Hold on. We need to set up a ward on the van so nothing gets stolen." Ash pulled a bottle from her bag and walked around the vehicle, sprinkling a fine dust onto the windows and doors.

"Cast it together?" Ember asked, reaching a hand toward her.

"No." Ash returned the empty bottle to her bag. "We need to save our vim, so we can break the ward on the auction house. Miles? Shade, are you up to it yet?"

"I'm good." Shade clutched Miles's hand, and they recited the spell aloud. The energy around us thickened, dancing across my skin, before they focused it on the van. They were strong witches, but their power wasn't nearly as potent as the Holland sisters'.

The fact didn't seem to bother them in the slightest.

We made our way inside the hotel, and I sat on a small sofa next to my witch while my brother worked his magic with Ash. Resting my arm on the back of the couch, I pinched Ember's neck, massaging the tension from her muscles.

She sighed, sinking farther into the cushion and closing her eyes for a long blink. "When we get to the room, can you research the people in charge of the auction? We need to know if they employed a witch to put the ward on the building or if they're witches themselves."

Miles patted his laptop bag. "I'll see what I can find."

"We've got a few hours before the auction starts, and I want us to be as prepared as possible." She touched my hand and scooted away. "I'm good. Thanks."

Ash smiled triumphantly as she approached, holding up two small pieces of plastic. "That was easy. Big Oil Boyd is staying in the penthouse. Come on."

We followed them to the elevator, and Ash tapped the card against a small box inside before pressing a button engraved with the letter P. It lit up, and the doors slid shut.

The elevator ascended rapidly, making my stomach feel as though it would slam into my pelvis. Pressure in my head built, and as I moved my jaw, my ears popped. A ding echoed through the small space, and the doors opened, revealing a large room with paintings and ornately framed mirrors hanging from alabaster walls.

A scent reminiscent of cloves and ginger filled the air, and glorious silence hung like a warm blanket over us, putting me at ease. Three closed doors indicated multiple rooms in the penthouse, and a large archway opened into the shared living area.

"This way." Ash motioned for us to follow her through the arch. "Can you believe this is considered one room? It's bigger than our apartment. It even has three bedrooms!"

"I can't believe you got the penthouse." Ember stood in the center of the room, turning in a circle. "I told you not to get greedy."

Ash shrugged. "It was Chaos's idea. I mean, we're already stealing from them. Why not go all out?"

"Room service will be delivering six steak dinners in half an hour." My brother wrapped an arm around his witch's waist and kissed the side of her head.

Ash leaned into him, resting a hand on his chest. Why could she accept their bond so easily, yet Ember fought ours? I needed a moment alone with Chaos to find out how he did it.

"Steak?" Ember rested her hands on her hips. "If Hecate hasn't already abandoned us, she sure as hell will now. How can you say eating steak is for the greater good?"

I sank onto the loveseat and stretched my arms across the back. "You almost died today. A Formorian nearly drained every ounce of life from your body to resurrect a long-extinct species that has no business in this realm or any other...and I will never forgive myself for allowing it to happen."

She crossed her arms, shifting her weight to one leg and jutting out her right hip. "A: You didn't allow anything. George...or Donal, or whatever the hell he called himself, was a tricky little wart of a man. And B: What does steak have to do with that?"

"We all need to replenish our strength if we're to retrieve the amulet and save the realm...you and Shade especially."

She opened her mouth to argue further but closed it instead, blowing a hard breath through her nose before her demeanor shifted. "I suppose I could use some protein. Miles, have you found anything about the auction house on the witchy web?"

I had been so engrossed in watching Ember's fiery protest, I didn't notice Miles setting up his computer at a table behind the sofa. Shade sat next to him, his gaze glued to the screen as Miles's fingers flew across the keys. How he typed so quickly, I couldn't fathom. I'd seen the keyboard on both the computer and a phone, and the letters were arranged in a nonsensical order.

Miles's mouth tightened, his eyes darting back and

forth as he read the screen. Shade swiped a hand down his face and leaned back in his chair while Chaos and Ash sank onto yet another sofa adjacent to the empty one.

Ember, my feisty little witch, could not sit still. She shifted her weight from side to side four times before assuming her normal pacing. "What is it? I don't like the way your faces look."

Miles inhaled deeply and raked a hand through his hair. "The auction tonight is for magical artifacts. It'll be swarming with witches."

"Wh...what?" Her expression was incredulous. "The site we looked at yesterday didn't mention anything about magic."

He hit a few more keys. "That was the public-facing website. Most of the time, their auctions are mundane. I had no idea..."

"How, then, did Boyd gain entry?" I leaned forward, my body feeling as antsy as Ember looked.

Miles rubbed his forehead. "When I created his fake online persona, I mentioned he had an interest in the occult. I guess that was enough. Unless..."

He slid his finger across the trackpad and typed something. "It's possible whoever set this up used a spell to make today's auction invisible to the mundane. Everyone there might be magical."

"Why did the site appear to be mundane when you registered?" I asked.

Miles shrugged. "A failsafe? Maybe the person running it didn't trust the spellcaster, so they made it look mundane just in case a human saw it. Who knows?"

"I better get started on the potions." Ash rose and carried her bag to a countertop on the far wall. Above it, a glass-door cabinet held multiple bottles of liquor, and crystal chalices occupied a shelf to the right.

"It's okay." Ember paced faster. "This is okay. It could be a good thing. Witches, beasties, demons, I can handle. This is a good thing."

"How so?" I tried to keep a neutral expression, but my brows crept upward and my lips pulled into a smile of their own volition. I adored watching the gears turn in her mind.

"It's good because..." Before she could finish, a buzzer sounded from the hall and a man's voice called through an intercom.

"Room service."

CHAPTER 5

EMBER

Ash pressed a button on the wall, unlocking the elevator door, and an attendant pushed in a linen-draped cart with six plates covered in silver domes.

"Can I get you anything else?" He clasped his gloved hands in front of his chest.

"Shit. A tip," I said under my breath. "He wants a tip." And I'd spent every dollar I had *and* maxed out my credit card. If we made it out of this alive, I had no idea how I'd recover. Maybe I could sell feet pictures on one of those fetish apps. I cringed at the thought.

"I've got it." Shade rose and handed the man a folded bill. "Thanks."

"Thank you, sir." The man bowed and returned to the elevator.

Miles closed his laptop and set it on the counter

before joining the rest of us at the table. Ash passed out the plates, and the moment I took the lid off mine, the savory scents of seared beef and black peppercorn wafted to my senses. My stomach growled on cue.

The steak was so tender, it practically melted on my tongue, and the buttery green beans with rosemary roasted potatoes tasted like heaven. I didn't realize how hungry I was until I finished my plate and gorged myself on three dinner rolls.

When we finished, Ash returned our plates to the cart and rolled it out of the room. "What's the new plan?" she asked as she returned. "We can't let another witch get their hands on the amulet. They might know how to use it."

I leaned back in my chair and tapped a finger against my lips. "I'm not sure we need a new one."

"How so?" she returned to her potion station and sprinkled dried oregano into a bowl while Miles opened his laptop.

"The auction protocol will be the same," he said. "The only difference will be the wards. I'm sure they'll be using magic to guard the relics in addition to firepower."

"Less firepower than they would have at a mundane auction, I'll bet." I drummed my fingers on the table. "Not only that, but if any humans are there, they already know magic is real. If it goes south, we can use our powers openly. This is good. Finally, something is going our way."

"Mmm..." Ash pressed her lips into a thin line.

I flattened my hand on the table. "What?"

"They know artifacts can be magical." She poured a potion into a bottle and corked it. "I doubt they've witnessed someone shoot flames from her fingertips."

"So I'll say I have an artifact that gives me fire power." I rose and rested my hands on my demon's shoulders. "It'll be fine. We've got this, right, Mayhem?"

"Indeed, we do." He clasped my hand, angling his head to look up at me. "Together, we can accomplish any feat."

His words warmed my chest and made my stomach tighten. At least the moths had settled. "We go in as planned. Big Oil Boyd and his plus one will ask to see the amulet ahead of the auction. While I'm charming the guards with my mad people skills, Mayhem will slip the stone into his pocket, and then we'll jet."

"Hecate, help us," Shade said. "You don't have people skills."

"I do when I want to." I crossed my arms. "Do you have a better idea?"

"I do, actually." He stood and joined Miles at the counter, leaning his hip against it. "I'll go with you."

I barked a laugh. "You think you're better with people than me? Please."

"Ember and I can handle it." Mayhem stood next to me. "We don't require assistance."

Shade bristled, squaring his shoulders toward us. "Like you didn't 'require assistance' at the Formorian's shop?" He made air quotes.

My nostrils flared with my hard exhale. "We'd have been fine if Ash hadn't said my name."

"Sure. Blame it on your sister like you always do." He crossed his arms. "Poor, incompetent Ash. Always the scapegoat. How convenient."

Mayhem tensed beside me. "The *assistance* you provided made you a liability. If it hadn't been for Miles, you'd have bled out on the floor."

"Stop it. All of you." Ash spread her fingers and shot three separate flames.

One hit Mayhem in the mouth as he tried to speak. He pushed it out with his tongue and sent it back to Ash. Another hit me on the cheek, the impact stinging before my skin absorbed the fire.

The third she directed at Shade, the flame singeing him before she called it back.

"Ow!" He clutched his neck where she'd burned him. "What the hell was that for? You know I'm not fireproof."

"Your arguing is giving me a headache. Keep it up, and I'll burn the whole building down." Her eyes narrowed, her brow lower than I'd ever seen. Something about her expression reminded me of a wild animal that had been backed into a corner and was ready to lash out against its foe.

She looked downright feral.

The sigil on her arm glowed a deep red, and the tension in her jaw eased, the vein near her temple no longer protruding. I glanced at Chaos. He kept his gaze trained on my sister, but the worry in his eyes was unmistakable.

She exhaled, her posture returning to normal, her expression softening to neutral before she scrunched her brows. "Why is everyone staring at me?"

Shade laughed dryly. "I wonder."

"I remember seeing a burn salve in Ash's bag." Miles rummaged through the satchel and pulled out a jar of blue goo.

"Who got burned?" She looked perplexed.

I made eye contact with Chaos and then Mayhem. Concern etched lines into their foreheads.

"You don't remember?" Mayhem asked.

"Remember what?" She corked another bottle. "What's going on? You're all acting weird."

"You burned Shade to stop their arguing." Miles spread the salve over Shade's neck and returned the jar to the bag.

Ash shook her head. "No, I didn't."

"You did." I walked toward her cautiously. When

she didn't bristle, I pressed my hand to her forehead. What I was looking for, I couldn't say. Did curses cause fevers?

Her skin felt a normal temperature, so I dropped my arm at my side. "You said you'd burn the building down if we didn't stop."

"I..." Her mouth hung open for a beat or two. "Oh, no."

"I was able to calm you through our bond." Chaos moved to her side and wrapped an arm around her waist. "You'll be fine, as long as we're together."

"It can't be the curse." She returned to her herbs, her hands trembling as she mixed another potion. "Mayhem must have..."

"I did nothing." He grasped my hand, and this time, I let him hold me. The familiar pinpricks danced across my skin, sending a warm jolt to my heart.

"We must obtain the rest of the amulet before your hysterics..." He cleared his throat. "Before the curse takes such hold that Chaos cannot control you."

"We'll take care of you." I lifted our entwined hands for emphasis. "Don't worry." Because I was worrying enough for all of us. If we lost my sister to the curse because I couldn't get my act together and lead this coven, I'd...

Well, I'd be dead. We all would.

Ash swallowed hard, her eyes glistening as if she held back tears. "I know you'll do your best."

I would from here on out. No more arguing with Mayhem or Shade or anyone else. No more letting my ego get in the way. I would keep myself in check, give it my best, and hope it would be good enough...which I should have been doing all along.

"Shade, what was your idea?" Chaos asked. "I assume you planned to go in under shadow because Boyd is only registered to bring one guest."

"Exactly." Shade straightened, turning toward Mayhem and me. "I'll follow you in, under shadow, and both of you can distract the guards long enough for me to swipe the amulet."

I shrugged, reminding myself he was just as capable of stealing a heavily guarded, eons-old amulet as I was. More so, thanks to his inborn power. "I suppose that could work too."

Miles, who had been clicking away on the keyboard, stopped typing. "That's the best idea I've heard so far. People will see your faces. You're the High Priestess of Salem, so they might recognize you. It's best if you aren't the one to commit the crime."

"I'm only the acting High Priestess. Most covens don't have a clue about our situation, and once we get my family back, I won't be in charge anymore." And thank the goddess for that.

"You're part of the governing bloodline, Em. Our pictures are on the witchy web." Ash bottled the last potion and carried her supplies to the wet bar sink.

"You'll have to go in as you, married to Boyd, another fire witch."

"Is his aura shroud still strong enough to fool them?" I rested my hand on his biceps.

"A Formorian prince believed he was a witch," Chaos said. "I can't imagine a witch less powerful than you seeing through it."

I caught my bottom lip between my teeth, chewing on it as I tugged from Mayhem's grasp, and resumed pacing. "One: Donal was tricky. Who knows if he saw through it or not? And two: Mayhem just had one foot...or hoof...in the Underworld. Guys, can you see through the shroud?"

Shade narrowed his eyes at my demon. "Yes, but we've known what he was from the get-go. I could always see through it."

"No, you couldn't." Miles turned away from his computer. "You were in awe at how well the spell worked, remember? You mentioned it after..." He flicked his gaze down before returning it to Shade. "You mentioned it."

Shade pressed his lips into a thin line and sighed. "Yeah. You're right, but I can see through it now. Can't you?"

Miles nodded.

"Did you bring all the ingredients for the spell?" I asked as Ash rummaged through her bag again.

She set a jar of lady's mantel next to the marjoram

and cinnamon oil. "I have everything but wolfsbane. I'll need to buy some."

"Okay, next steps." I grabbed the bag I'd packed with my dress and shoes for the event and slung the new one a la Donal's store over my arm. "Ash, you and Chaos find a metaphysical shop and get everything you think we'll need. Shade, did you bring anything to wear besides spandex?"

"No, but I'll be in shadow the whole time."

"Unless something happens and you can't hold it." I strode toward the hallway that led to the bedrooms, pausing at the entrance. "Go with Ash and Chaos and get something dressy enough that you'll look like you belong there...just in case."

He nodded. "I can do that."

"Miles..." I said.

"I'll stay here and get it set up. We'll need to be within a block of the auction house half an hour before the doors open."

"Good. I'm going to shower and get ready to be a trophy wife." I shuddered at the thought. Though not at being Mayhem's wife, surprisingly. That idea sat unnaturally well in my psyche. It was the trophy part that made me want to wretch.

"I'm unfamiliar with the term 'trophy wife,'" Mayhem said, following me through the bedroom into the en suite bathroom, which was bigger than my entire bed and bath combo at home.

"It basically means a wife whose only value is being arm candy." I grabbed a velvet hanger for my new dress and hung it from a hook near the door.

"Arm candy?"

"She looks good on his arm, but he doesn't give a flying flip about who she is on the inside." I gazed into the massive mirror above the sink. The small bit of mascara I'd applied in the morning had run, rimming my eyes in faded black. My hair looked like both a squirrel and a dove had nested on my head, and my shirt was torn and bloodied. I couldn't say whose blood it was. Shade's maybe? Or mine?

"Ew." I curled my lip at my reflection. "I'm definitely not arm candy."

Mayhem picked up a wide-toothed comb and began working the knots out of my hair. "But you are a trophy."

"Excuse me?" I spun and grabbed his wrist. "Care to elaborate?"

He searched my eyes, his gaze traveling to my lips for a moment before he spoke, "I treasure you, Ember. If I could win your heart the way you've won mine, it would be my greatest accomplishment."

I opened my mouth to argue that I was not a prize to be won, but I couldn't force the words from my throat. That silent vow I'd made to stop arguing with him included this too. It was time to stop deflecting and accept the emotions churning inside me. All of them.

"Why do you treasure me?" I asked.

He blinked as if my question surprised him, but he recovered quickly, one side of his mouth pulling into a teasing grin. "Aside from your value as candy on my arm?"

"Aside from that." I turned on the shower, letting the hot water fill the bathroom with steam. It smelled fresh, like lavender and sandalwood, and I kicked off my boots before stuffing my socks inside them.

"Allow me to count the reasons. You are intelligent, fierce, and feisty." He ticked them off on his fingers. "Despite your self-professed lack of people skills, you lead your coven with dignity and grace."

"I..." *No more arguing, Em. Keep your mouth shut and let the man flatter you. It's not that hard.*

I tugged my tattered shirt over my head, clicking my tongue at the rip. At least it was on the seam.

"What else?" I asked without making eye contact as I shoved my pants down my legs and stepped out of them.

He inhaled deeply, and I could imagine the primal look in his eyes, could feel the need forming between us. "You recognize the talents in others, and you encourage their strengths rather than envy them. It's a lesson I am beginning to learn, thanks to you."

I held my hand beneath the water, adjusting the temperature to a nearly searing heat. The biggest showerhead hung from the ceiling, the flow coming down like rain in the center of the massive, tiled stall. Six other jets lined three walls, and I turned them on as well.

"All that's missing is the rotating scrubber brush, and we'd have ourselves a human car wash." I choked off a maniacal giggle.

"You're doing it again," he said, and I turned around to find his shirt and pants folded neatly on the counter. "Every time I bring up our bond, you make jokes. Stop it."

"I, umm..." I swallowed hard, unclasping my bra and letting it fall to the floor. I could do this. I could let myself feel. "Please continue. Why else do you treasure me?"

His pupils dilated until only a thin ring of purple remained. "When you love someone, you love deeply and completely, and if you will have me, I would be honored to love you the same way in return."

My tongue slipped out to lick my lips against my will, and his gaze locked on my mouth, making my stomach flutter.

"I am your soulmate, Ember. It's time you accept it." He slipped off his underwear and stepped past me, into the shower.

CHAPTER 6
MAYHEM

Silky water fell onto my head like rain, and I turned, allowing the side streams to massage my back as I waited for Ember to make her move. She stood there, staring at me, her gaze caressing the length of my body before she met my eyes.

How I longed for her hands to do the same.

"What if I'm not ready to accept it?" She arched a brow, crossing her arms and drawing my attention to her hardened nipples.

Not that I needed a visual cue to her arousal. I could smell the pheromones rising to the surface of her skin, sweet and spiced, like orange blossoms and cinnamon.

With a deep inhale, I stepped out of the stream and

rested a hand on the glass divider. "You don't strike me as a woman who enjoys wasting time."

"We both know I don't. What's your point?" She tilted her head, jutting out her chin in a show of stubbornness.

I exhaled sharply. "Do you not grow tired of these games?"

Her lips parted as if she would respond, but she pressed them together, screwing them to one side in an adorable manner.

"My point is we have a limited amount of time to satisfy our urges, so we should take full advantage of this glorious showering room before we must return to our quest." I held out my hand to her.

"That's a good point." She slipped off her panties and placed her hand in mine.

Before she could change her mind, I pulled her into the shower and shoved her back against the glass, pressing my body to hers and pinning her arms above her head. She gasped at my forcefulness, but her hooded eyes and ghost of a smile told me she enjoyed letting go of control.

I trailed my tongue from her collarbone to her ear, nipping the lobe between my teeth. Goosebumps rose on her skin, and a breathy moan escaped her lips.

"If I had my way, I'd keep you here until our skin turned to prunes and our bodies ached from exhaustion." I released her wrists and glided my hands down her arms to hold her face. "Then I would carry you to bed and make love to you again."

"That sounds..." With her gaze on my lips, she inclined her chin, nearly begging me to kiss her as she wrapped her arms around my shoulders. "That sounds like a good time."

"Indeed." I took her mouth with mine, parting her lips with my tongue and tangling it with hers. My arousal grew, and I reached down to adjust it, pressing my length against her stomach. The feel of her soft skin on my shaft made me shudder, and my demon rose to just below the surface, the tips of my horns protruding from my scalp, begging me to release my natural form.

"Our team will return soon," I whispered against her lips. "I need you with such urgency, I don't think I can hold back."

"It's not..." She pressed her lips together and leaned back to look at me, sliding her fingers into my hair to caress my horns. She searched my eyes, the moment agonizingly long before she finally said, "I want *you* to take me. The real you."

I stepped away from her, my brow lowering as I held her gaze, my talons extending from my fingertips as my hands morphed into their natural form. My horns grew, arching upward while my tusks length-ened. "You can't possibly want me like this."

"No." She ran a finger over my sigil on her arm, making me shiver. "Not like this. Not halfway."

My pulse quickened, my heart thudding in my chest, threatening to burst as I transformed. I grew in height and girth. My skin turned its natural shade of purple-gray, and my feet morphed into hooves. "I've never taken a mortal like this."

She stepped toward me, resting her hands against my chest and peering up, into my eyes. "I'll be your first, last, and always."

Her quick intake of air said her words had surprised her as much as they delighted me. She ran a finger down my chest, stopping just above my cock. "But let's get one thing straight. It's *my* team. Not ours."

A growl rumbled in my chest. With my demon free and my senses heightened, I could hold back no more. I grabbed her shoulders and spun her around, pressing her back against the wall.

"You belong to me, witch. Everything you have is mine...is ours to share." I withdrew my talons and reached between her legs, thrusting two fingers inside her.

She gasped and then moaned, her lids fluttering before she locked her gaze on mine. "That's not..."

I moved my fingers out and thrust them deeper inside her. "You belong to me, as I belong to you. Everything I have is yours."

I kissed her as hard as I dared in this form and pulled my fingers out to caress her clit. "We are but two halves of one being. Together, we are whole. Apart, I am nothing."

She sucked in a shaky breath, leaning her head back against the wall and fighting to keep her eyes open. "I think... I think you're right. I think this is right."

She held my face in her hands and pressed her lips to mine, her tongue darting between my tusks and making me lose control.

I wrapped my arms around her, holding her as tightly as her mortal form would allow, but even with her bare skin against me, I couldn't hold her close enough. "I love you, Ember. My soul has loved yours since the beginning of my existence."

"I think..." She pulled back to look into my eyes. "No, I don't think. I know I love you too. My soul loves yours."

My knees nearly buckled beneath me. I never knew how badly I needed to hear those words until that moment. So many emotions that I couldn't begin to define rose inside me, swirling and pulsing, tightening my throat and causing my chest to ache. Pressure built in my eyes, the overwhelming sensation of loving Ember—and being loved in return—threatening to escape as tears.

I turned her around, lest she witness my display of

weakness, and grasped her hands, pressing them against the wall. My dick throbbed, aching to fill her as she leaned her hips toward me.

Pressing my tip against her folds, I rubbed the head up and down her slit, gathering moisture on my shaft before slowly sliding inside her. "I don't want to hurt you."

"You won't. We were made for each other." She reached behind me and grasped my ass. "But I do want to watch."

She leaned toward the far wall, and we turned as one until we could see ourselves in the mirror above the sink. Her fair skin appeared so delicate, her frame minuscule compared to mine.

"You're magnificent," she said, smiling at our reflection.

"You are a work of wonder." I slid out and in, making her sigh and moan in unison.

The wall jets blasted against her, and she angled the top one away so she could lean closer to the wall. I reached around her and aimed the lower one between her legs, the sensation making her cry out in pleasure.

"Oh, gods." She adjusted her stance, giving both me and the water better access to her center. "Do it slow."

I followed her command, sliding in and out in slow, fluid strokes while she watched my movements in the mirror. As her breathing quickened, I increased my speed, and when she gasped and screamed my name, I slammed into her, holding her against the stream as she writhed in ecstasy.

But I wasn't finished with her yet.

Her orgasm peaked and subsided, and she angled the jet away to lean her forearms against the wall. "Holy Hecate."

I slipped out of her, turning her around to face me. "I love that I can make you invoke your goddess's name with my cock."

She laughed. "You've got an impressive one. Wow."

"We aren't finished." I brushed her wet hair from her forehead. "I want to look into your eyes the next time you come. I can take you to the bed or do it here."

"Here is good." She swallowed hard.

"I didn't hurt you?"

"Not at all, but I might have to climb you." She clutched my dick and stroked it twice before gripping my shoulders. "Help me up?"

"With pleasure." I grabbed her ass and lifted her, settling her onto my shaft as she wrapped her legs around me. The sensation of her tight, velvet sheath enveloping me made me groan.

With my demon strength and her small frame, it felt as if she weighed no more than a feather. But I wasn't sure my knees would hold me when I found my release. Ember, this witch...this goddess...loved me.

The real me. I had never experienced such elation in all of my existence.

I stepped out of the shower and carried her to the countertop, never breaking our intimate union as I set her down and leaned my hands against the surface. I had to bend, due to my height in this form, but my hooves gripped the slickened tiles, giving me enough leverage to thrust into her.

Over and over.

I glanced at my reflection as I pleasured her. My pupils had turned to pinpricks, the purple in my irises rippling with gray. She slid her hands upward to caress my horns with her fingertips.

"You're beautiful," she whispered, her expression turning to one of ecstasy.

"As are you." I plunged deeper inside her, my rhythm growing stronger, faster.

She dug her nails into my back, dragging them downward as she came once more. Her sounds, her scent, her everything consumed me, and I lost myself to her.

The orgasm ripped through my body, shredding my cells and reforming them as Ember mastered me. This woman knew me. Every part of my body, every thought in my mind. She anticipated my every move, she knew me...and she loved me.

If heaven existed, I had taken up permanent residence there, right in this moment.

She ran her hands over my skin and gazed at my face, completely unafraid, unappalled at my appearance. What had I done to deserve this woman? Nothing, except to place a curse on her bloodline. What had the Fates been thinking when they wove this tapestry?

Their plan wasn't mine to question, so I would simply enjoy it, revel in it, until the bitter end.

My breathing slowed in time with hers, and I pulled out, still resting my hands on the countertop and leaning toward her. She gazed into my eyes and smiled.

"As much as I love seeing you like this, we better put your demon away and finish our shower." She kissed my cheeks before pressing her lips to mine. "Our team will be back soon."

CHAPTER 7
EMBER

Holy mother of magic. The past hour or so had felt surreal. *Un*real. If not for the pleasant ache between my thighs, I would've assumed I'd dreamed it. Yet, there I was, standing across the counter from the demon I loved, smiling like a fool.

He winked, and my stomach fluttered. How the simple movement of his eyelid could affect my insides like that baffled me, but hey… I'd just let him do me in his demon form. My mind was scrambled at the moment.

The weirdest thing? I hadn't just let him. I'd *wanted* him in his demon form. Me. In love with a full-on demon. Hecate have mercy.

"I'm glad you had a good time while we were gone." Ash bumped her hip to mine, drawing me from my trance. She held the aura-shrouding powder in both hands and offered one fistful to me. "But it's time to get this shit show on the road."

"What makes you think we had a good time?" I held out my hand, and she poured the powder into my palm, laughing.

"Neither of you has stopped smiling since I walked in. Ready?"

"Let's do it." I held her free hand, and we recited the incantation in unison. "Aura strong, magic deep, we hide your essence from all who seek."

We blew the powder onto my demon, and he inhaled deeply, his conspiratorial smirk never slipping as the magic took hold, hiding his demonic nature.

At least, I assumed it was hidden. Thanks to the sigil glowing softly on my arm, I continued to feel his true self. A self I loved.

Crazy, I know.

"Guys, did it work?" Ash asked.

Miles squinted at Mayhem, and Shade sauntered toward him, his eyes calculating as he circled him. "If I didn't already know what he is, I wouldn't have a clue."

"Same." Miles closed his laptop and slid it into his bag. "All three of you look the part. Getting inside won't be an issue, and Shade, you'll blend right in if you have to drop your shadow."

"Here. To fireproof your dress, just in case." Ash

handed me a tiny spray bottle filled with sunny yellow liquid. "Who would've thought a group of light witches...Veil Keepers, no less...would team up with demon princes to rob an auction?"

I sprayed my front before handing it to her so she could coat what little fabric there was on the back of my slinky little dress. "At this point—with what we've been through the past few months—nothing surprises me. And anyway..."

I tested the hem of my dress, trying to singe the threads. They refused to burn. Good. "It's not like we don't have experience in theft and breaking and entering. This ain't our first rodeo. Is it, Boyd?" I winked at my demon, and he smiled.

"No, ma'am, it ain't. I only wish I could have joined you on your previous adventures."

"You're here now. That's what matters." I slipped on my kitten heels and sprayed them with the fire-proofing potion. "What do you think?" I turned in a circle for Mayhem to see.

"You look stunning, as always." He put on a black sports coat and adjusted his bolo tie. "I, on the other hand, look ridiculous."

"You look like a Texas oil baron," Miles said. "It's perfect, though Ember, you'd look more convincing in higher heels."

I laughed. "You're lucky I'm not wearing combat

boots. If things go south, and we have to fight, I can't kick ass in stilettos."

"It's time." Chaos rested a hand on Ash's back.

"Everyone's clear on their duties?" Miles asked.

The energy in the room shifted, a heaviness settling on our shoulders as we nodded our agreement. We were about to attempt a heist.

An effing heist, for Hecate's sake!

Yeah, we had proficiency in theft, but our experience was in coven libraries and apartments of deceased, so-called friends. "A heavily guarded auction house," I muttered, not meaning to say it out loud.

Mayhem moved toward me, brushing a strand of hair from my forehead. "With you by my side, anything is possible. We can do this."

The conviction in his words made them almost believable.

"Shall we?" He held out his arm like a gentleman, and I laced mine around his biceps.

"Let's go rob an auction."

ASH DROVE, miraculously finding parking a block from our target. She left the engine running and turned in her seat to give me an encouraging smile. "You've got this. In and out, and no egos."

She gave each of us a pointed look before shaking

her head. "I don't know why I said that. We're sending in our three biggest."

"It's kind of like telling a wolf not to howl, isn't it?" I unbuckled my seat belt and cast a longing gaze at the hidey hole in the floorboard. I felt naked without my weapons. "We'll behave. I promise."

Mayhem rested his hand on my thigh. "We will do our best."

"Put your earpieces in so I can test them." Miles handed us a small box, and we each stuck the tiny pieces of silicon into our ears.

Mayhem and I climbed out of the van, and he slid the door shut behind us. Squinting, I peered through the tinted window. "Why isn't Shade coming?"

"He's standing right beside you." Mayhem gestured to my right.

"There are cameras all over the city," Shade's disembodied voice said. "It might look weird if I disappeared on screen."

"Testing," Miles said into our earpieces. "Can you hear me?"

"Loud and clear." I pressed my fingers to my ear.

"Don't do that," Ash's voice came through. "The whole point of them being small is so no one knows you're wearing them."

"Gotcha." I fisted my hands so I wouldn't do it again. What could I say? All the FBI and CIA and Secret

Service people did it in the movies. I'd learned a bad habit by watching a screen. Imagine that.

"Ready, guys?" I started down the sidewalk, toward the auction house. "Our mission, should we choose to accept it, is simple."

"Have we not already accepted the mission?" Mayhem asked, his expression adorably perplexed.

I laughed. "Yes, dear, we have. In, snag the amulet, and out. As tempting as it'll be to check out all the other artifacts they've gathered, we have to stay focused."

"Indeed." He held out his arm, and I clutched his biceps. "The sooner we obtain the amulet, the sooner we can return to our penthouse and utilize the plush mattress in the main suite."

Shade snorted somewhere to my left as we stepped into a crosswalk. A crisp autumn wind whipped down the street, blowing my hair into my face and raising goosebumps on my bare arms. I should've taken a shawl or a shrug from the store of doom, but oh well. Only fifty yards to go, and we'd be at the entrance.

"Have I told you how stunning you are?" Mayhem asked, his voice low.

"Don't get used to this look." I adjusted the top of my dress, fighting the urge to reach inside it to reposition my boobs. Bras had been around for over one hundred years, and no one had come up with a comfortable, strapless version that didn't slide down the first chance it got.

"Ash, when this is through, I've got a job for you and your sewing skills."

She laughed. "I'll get right on it. After I organize the library, figure out how to make spell capsules instead of bottles, and reopen the store so we can pay our bills."

"Add reinventing the strapless bra to your list." Because we *would* get through this. Ash would have plenty of time to whittle away at her to-dos because things would go back to normal. They had to, and I would keep telling myself that until they did.

We stopped in front of the building, a ten-story brick and glass structure with three sets of heavy double doors. No sign announced the name of the owner, but the magical vibration of the wards turned my skin to gooseflesh.

"Go ahead and powder the doors," I said, looking at my demon because I had no idea where Shade stood.

"It's already done. I'm going to grab your hand. Don't react." Warmth and pressure wrapped around my wrist before Shade slid his hand down to clutch mine.

I took Mayhem's hand. "The spell Ash concocted is temporary. It shouldn't set off any alarms, but we have to cross the ward immediately before it resets."

Mayhem opened his power to me, and I fought a gasp as the low vibration and pinpricking sensation traveled up my arm to spread through my body. I shared a little of it with Shade so we could cast this spell without draining our vim too much.

We recited the incantation together. "Ward of light, this is our plight. Peel away your hood so we may enter for the greater good."

The energy on the building wavered, the pressure of the ward lifting, blinking out. I tugged from Shade's grasp and held Mayhem's arm, ushering him toward the middle set of doors and praying to the goddess that this was the only ward on the auction.

"We're inside," I said, still fighting the urge to touch my earpiece and rearrange my boobs.

"Good," Miles replied. "Someone should approach you to check in."

"Oh, no. You clearly didn't read the rules of the auction." A witch in a dark gray suit and red stilettos clicked toward us, shaking her head and gesturing at what I could only imagine was Shade.

"Either drop your shadow or kindly leave the premises." She tapped her finger on a tablet screen and arched a brow.

Shade sighed heavily and appeared next to Mayhem.

The woman clicked her tongue. "No shadow magic, no weapons, no spells intended to affect the outcome of the auction. You received the rules via email after you registered, Mr...?

"I apologize, ma'am." Mayhem laid on a heavy Texas accent. "My name is Boyd Anderson, and this here is my wife, Ember."

She swiped the screen and tapped it three times. "Yes, you and your wife are registered."

"This is my assistant, Shade. His shadow has a mind of its own when he's nervous." He lowered his voice and winked. "He's kinda shy and as awkward as a nun in a whorehouse. Please forgive his transgression."

A blush spread across the woman's cheeks as she gazed into my demon's eyes, and I suddenly felt the urge to gouge out hers. Okay, I wouldn't really do that, and I knew he was charming her so we could complete our mission, but damn.

Jealousy was such an ugly emotion. I suppose I'd never cared about anyone enough to feel it before.

The woman cleared her throat. "He isn't on the list."

"Surely you can add him... I apologize again, ma'am. I missed your name." Mayhem stepped toward her, his gaze slipping to her mouth before returning to her eyes.

I bristled and clenched my teeth.

She swallowed audibly. "It's Hazel."

"Hazel, Shade is also my accountant, and I need

him present when I make large purchases. I plan to spend a lot of money today." He winked again, and my stomach tightened along with my jaw.

"Well…" She let out a breathy laugh. "We don't normally make exceptions, Mr. Anderson, but I see you've been verified as a platinum-level bidder. If I can see his ID, I'll add him to your registration."

The tendons in Shade's neck were so tight, you could've plucked them like guitar strings, and a vein on his temple looked like it was about to burst.

"Give it to her, Shade," Miles said through the coms. "It's not ideal, but we don't have a choice."

He dug his wallet from his jacket and offered her his ID. "I won't be bidding. Just assisting."

She scanned the barcode on the back of his license and returned it to him. "Thank you, sir. This way."

Her heels clicked on the tile as we followed her through the foyer. Mine clicked a little too, but the sound was lower, much more practical. Thudding boot heels would have been better.

"Stop fidgeting," Mayhem said under his breath. "You must appear confident in your clothing."

"You try feeling confident when your bra is about to slip down to your waist and take your boobs with it."

"The ladies' room is down that hall and to the right." Hazel gestured at a massive archway. "Men's is to the left."

My cheeks heated, but I kept following her. "Thank you."

The foyer opened into another room with squishy carpet and a ginormous crystal chandelier hanging from the center of the ceiling. Black and white photos of New York during various decades hung from the dark green walls, and a bar and buffet stood at the back of the space.

"Here, you will find refreshments, and you may pick up your auction paddle on your way to the main event." She tapped her screen and closed the cover before batting her eyes at Mayhem. "May I assist you in any other way?"

Oof. I did not like the way she said that. The emphasis she put on "any other" made her intention as clear as pure quartz.

"We're good. Thanks." I gripped Mayhem's arm and rested my hand on his chest.

"Actually..." Mayhem patted my shoulder. "I would like to see the amulet...item 457...ahead of the bidding. Can you make that happen?"

She glanced at me before smiling at him. "Absolutely. Someone will find you as soon as it's ready for viewing. Please, enjoy yourselves."

Shade laughed as she walked away. "Ember Holland finally met her match."

I blew a breath through my nose. "I could kick her ass with both hands cuffed behind my back."

"Oh, I don't doubt that." He laughed again. "But could you be any more jealous?"

I glared at Shade, trying to formulate a snippy comeback, but my mind blanked. Yes, I was jealous of a shadow witch because she flirted with my man. I could admit that.

Hell, she hadn't even flirted. Not really. Honestly, she hadn't done a damn thing wrong, but I could feel her attraction to my demon and I hated it. *Get a grip, Em.*

"You have nothing to worry about." Mayhem hooked a finger beneath my chin, lifting my gaze to meet his. "You are my first, last, and always, remember?"

"I remember." I rose onto my toes and brushed a gentle kiss to his lips before wiping the lipstick away with my thumb.

"Mr. Anderson?" A man in a dark red jacket approached us. "The item is ready to be viewed."

Hazel the shadow witch flanked him, her mouth tight, her eyes narrowed in a perturbed expression. "I'll be accompanying you this evening, unless your assistant would like to leave the premises."

A sense of smugness made me straighten my spine. Did our friend get into trouble for allowing Shade to stay? I started to think that was what she got for fawning over my man, but the direness of our circumstances sank in instead.

She'd be watching Shade's every move, so he was out of play. I should have anticipated something like this. They had guards with automatic rifles. Of course they would have people actively watching for shadows and spells. Honestly, I was surprised the ward on the building wasn't stronger. They hadn't even hired an elemental witch to cast it.

But now we had to go back to plan A: Me distracting the guards while Mayhem swiped the necklace. But Hazel would have one mesmerized eye on my demon too. *Shit.*

My pulse sprinted, and I took a deep breath, trying to look calm, but Miles's voice over the coms made my stomach take a flying leap into my throat. "All right, guys. It's go time."

CHAPTER 8

MAYHEM

I offered my arm to Ember and fought my smile as we followed Hazel and the guard toward the vault. The shadow witch not only couldn't hold a candle to my fire witch, but she could not ignite a single, minuscule spark inside me. No woman ever would for the rest of my existence.

I had to admit, though, watching Ember's subtle display of dominance added fuel to the already raging inferno of love and desire I felt for her.

We exited the refreshment area and turned left, passing through a second massive archway when a *ding-dong* sound echoed through the corridor. Hazel and the guard stopped short, her gaze snapping to his.

A moment later, a woman's voice sounded through the building's intercom. "Attention guests and staff.

Please gather in the waiting area until further notice. Code blue thirty-seven."

Hazel tried to hide her gasp by clearing her throat. "I'm sorry. We'll have to go back to the waiting area."

"What's blue thirty-seven?" Ember asked, crossing her arms.

"Go ahead. I'll bring them in." Hazel gestured at the guard, who turned on his heel and jogged toward the vault.

"We need to go back. Follow me." Her heels clicked on the floor, and another bell echoed before the voice repeated the instructions.

Ember widened her stance. "What's blue thirty-seven?"

Hazel turned toward her, wringing her hands, her gaze jumping from Ember to Shade to me before she leaned toward us and whispered, "There's been a security breach. I don't..." She shook her head and looked at Shade.

"Oh. Oh, hey..." Ember touched Hazel's elbow. "They wouldn't lock the place down over Shade. If they didn't want him here, they'd have made him leave."

"Yeah." She blew out a breath. "I just... I really need this job."

"Then let's make sure you keep it." Ember guided her toward the foyer, and Shade and I followed reluctantly.

The final piece of Lucifer's amulet lay a few yards away. Temptation to run for it, to obtain it by any means necessary, had my muscles tensing and my hands clenching into fists.

I could take it so effortlessly. Getting Ember and Shade out safely would not be as easy.

"What's happening?" Ash asked in my earpiece. "Do you see anyone suspicious?"

"Not as of yet," I replied quietly. "Perhaps your spell to pass through the ward set off an alarm after all."

"Not a chance," she said. "An arrogant, mid-level witch cast it, probably thinking no one would have the gall to attempt a heist at a magical auction in the most secure house in the country."

"She's right," Shade said. "The magic barely fought back. We didn't cause this."

We passed through the foyer and gathered with the other attendees in the carpeted room. I scanned the faces of those present, searching for a sign of the culprit. "Hazel, how many shadow witches are working tonight? Could someone else have sneaked in the way Shade did?"

"There are six of us stationed around the building. Two of us manned check-in, but I don't see Misty anywhere now." She tugged her phone from her pocket and tapped the screen. "Her tracker is off."

"There's your security breach," Ember said. "Does she practice dark magic?"

"No." Hazel shook her head adamantly. "We went through an intense screening process to get these jobs. We had aura readings, one-on-one interviews, personality tests, and mundane background checks. Plus we all had to pass through the ward to get into the building."

Ember spun in a circle, her eyes calculating. "Wards can be dissolved."

"Not without setting off an alarm." She pressed her phone to her ear. "Misty, are you okay? Call me."

"Powerful witches can..." I began, but Ember's sharp look made me stop mid-sentence.

Hazel let out a nervous laugh. "Okay, but who here is that strong? It would take an elemental to break it quietly."

I arched a brow at Ember. It seemed our new friend didn't know she stood in the presence of a Holland witch. We would have to keep it that way.

"All guests are accounted for," the voice over the intercom said. "Initiate seven-five-seven."

"Oh, this is bad." Hazel squinted at her phone. "Better get comfortable."

I was about to inquire why when a pair of men with large guns closed the doors to the foyer. The *thunk* of a massive lock engaging echoed in the room, and the crowd's incessant chatter quieted to a murmur.

"What's happening?" both Ember and Ash on the earpiece asked in unison.

Hazel jerked her head toward an empty corner of the room. "Come over here. I'm not supposed to talk about it."

We followed her, and I picked up a pastry from the buffet on our way, shoving the entire thing into my mouth. The cream cheese center meshed perfectly with the tart lemon frosting.

Ember blinked at me and shook her head.

Hazel motioned for us to get closer. "Seven-five-seven is a lock-down protocol. We're stuck here until they verify all the artifacts are safe and they find the culprit. They'll interview each of us separately."

Her gaze darted about the room, her brows drawing inward until deep wrinkles formed above the bridge of her nose. "I can't stay in here. I have... I have a job to do."

Ember closed her eyes and pressed her fingers to her temples. "We don't have time for this to turn into an Agatha Christie novel." She looked at me. "What should we do?"

I had no answer of which the team would approve.

"At least we have food. It could be a long night, so we might as well settle in." Hazel shoved her phone into her pocket, her nervous expression contrasting the calmness of her words.

"You have to find a way out," Ash said. "Miles is tapping into your phones to track you, and then he'll guide you to the amulet."

"The—" Ember began before making a face at me. We couldn't speak freely while Hazel remained within earshot.

"How's your vim?" Shade asked, sensing the issue. "It must be draining to use your active power of seeing through shadow for so long."

Hazel laughed dryly. "Right? I'll have to sleep for three days to recover."

With Shade distracting the guard dog, Ember and I stepped away and settled at a small table far from the crowd and any other prying ears.

"There are armed guards at all the exits," Ember whispered. "We aren't going anywhere without causing a scene."

"Perhaps a scene is exactly what we need." I drummed my fingers on the table. "If the crowd were to break out in a mass panic, we could slip out the door during their distraction."

"Absolutely not." Ember laid her hand on mine, stopping my drumming.

"That could work," Ash said, at least one sister agreeing with me.

"How many people would we inadvertently kill if

Mayhem did his thing in here? For once, violence isn't the answer." Ember squeezed my fingers and let them go. "We can't make these people start fighting each other, especially not with all the assault rifles in the room."

"Are you trying to convince me or yourself?" I asked.

"Both. As much as I'd loved to kick some ass right now, we can't be the cause of anyone else's death. I'm done leaving a trail of bodies in our wake."

A *clunk* sounded from above, and the chandelier rattled, turning lopsided before swinging violently from its base. A shimmering disturbance dropped to the floor, and a man let out a gurgling scream.

I rose to my feet. "It appears we have our distraction."

CHAPTER 9
EMBER

"Please tell me that's not what I think it is," I shouted over the blood-curdling screams as I scanned the room, searching for anything I could use as a weapon.

"It's the fae. They're here for the amulet." Shade said as he rushed toward me.

"No shit, Captain Obvious." I grabbed a handful of fruit kabobs from the buffet, but the wooden skewers were as light as balsa sticks. If steel broke upon impact with giant insect armor, these would turn to splinters. I shoved a melon ball into my mouth and tossed the rest into a yogurt bowl.

"What is happening?" Hazel pressed a hand to her chest and backed up until she smacked the wall. Her gaze bounced around the room, her brow furrowing in concentration as if she were attempting to see through shadows that didn't exist.

"Those are fae." A growl rumbled from Mayhem's chest, and his talons protruded from his fingertips.

I grasped his hands, covering his built-in Freddy Krueger knives, and whispered, "Put those away, Wolverine."

He growled again, but he did as I asked. "We have no weapons."

"Yes, we do." Shade tossed me a butter knife he'd snagged from the buffet. It had a rounded tip and a dull blade, but it was better than the fruit skewer I'd found.

"What the hell?" a man shouted.

"I can't see them," another one said.

A woman slammed against the wall, her throat collapsing before her stomach ripped open. Her insides spilled onto the floor as the invisible fae wrenched out her liver. The crowd silenced, watching in sheer horror, the sounds of bones breaking and flesh tearing echoing through the room as the soldier plunged his claws into her chest and ripped out her heart, *Indiana Jones and the Temple of Doom* style.

The squelching and munching that followed made me gag, but the gasps of terror from the other witches spurred me into action.

"Where's the rift?" I shoved the knife into my bra and finally adjusted my boobs. I was tempted to whip the damn thing off, but it was the only clothing I had on that could hold a weapon.

"Above the chandelier." Mayhem pointed, and another shimmery *Predator* monster dropped onto the fixture. "I count three."

"Three rifts?" I grabbed more butter knives, creating a bouquet of blades in my cleavage.

"Three soldiers." He gathered fire in his palms. "Make that four."

"How?" Hazel's eyes grew to the size of salad plates.

Mass panic ensued, making the spacious buffet room feel like a tiny, overcrowded closet. Grunts, rips, screams, and gurgling last breaths created a cacophony of horror as the fae wreaked their havoc on the unsuspecting witches.

"This was a setup." I clutched two metal shrimp skewers and kicked off my shoes, scanning the room for the telltale shimmer of overgrown flies.

To my left, someone shouted a binding spell. I waited for a fae to freeze—or hell, I'd have been happy if it affected the entire room—but no magic built in the air. Her words were as mundane as a vampire was thirsty.

"We could use your spell kit about now, Ash." I pressed my fingers to the earpiece, not giving a flying flip if anyone knew I was wired. "We've got a rift and four fae that need freezing."

"Magic won't work in here." Hazel eyed Mayhem's fiery hands. "It shouldn't work."

I ignited a fireball, heating the metal skewers until they glowed red. "What do you mean?"

"I guess they didn't count on elementals." She poked at her phone screen, frowning. "Once you pass the foyer, there's a ward to bind magic on every room. No one can cast a spell, but apparently, elementals can use their inborn gifts."

"She's right," Shade said. "Shadows aren't elemental. I can't create one."

"There should be a door in the back left corner, hidden in the wall," Ash said over the coms. "If you can get through it, we can guide you out."

A guard blasted his assault rifle into the chandelier. The bullets lodged in—or passed through—the ceiling, but glass rained onto the throng of witches, making them panic more. The fifth fae, who'd dropped through the rift at just the right time, took a hit in the neck. He screeched, his shroud slipping as he thudded on the floor, revealing his ghastly nature to the crowd.

"Find the door, Em," Ash reminded me.

"We'll get right on that." I stormed toward the injured fae, elbowing people out of my way and shoving a shrimp skewer into his ear hole. The bug goo inside him sizzled with my heat, and I lifted a layer of his armor and jabbed a butter knife into his heart.

Another fae grabbed the guard with the rifle and

hurled him upward, into the ceiling. Sheetrock cracked and bones crunched before he fell, smacking the floor. Blood oozed from a gash in his head, and I cringed as the fae tossed him onto his back and ripped out his organs.

Rising to my feet, I spun toward Hazel. "Can you lift the ward? These witches aren't fighters. Without their spell powers, they'll be massacred."

A fae shimmered three feet behind her, and Mayhem hurled hellfire at him. The bastard screeched, losing his glamour for half a second as he backed away to find an easier target.

Hazel squealed and clutched Mayhem's arm. "I can't. I didn't cast it, and even if I was strong enough to break it, my magic doesn't work in here either."

"Hecate on a hellhound. Your people didn't think this through. You've trapped us in a barrel. We're the fish, and the fae have the guns."

"Get to the door, Em," Ash said in my ear. "I'll see if I can lift the wards from the foyer."

"Don't you dare come into this building." I grabbed Hazel by the arm, dragging her to the door in question. "Open it."

"I can't." She blubbered, tears streaming down her face. "The seven-five-seven protocol means the doors are bolted by the security system. Only an admin can unlock them."

"Miles?" I asked.

"On it." The sound of his fingers clicking keys filled my ear. "Ash is on her way inside. I tried to stop her, but you know how those two are."

Yes, I knew all too well, and I couldn't fault her. Had our roles been reversed, and she'd ordered me to stay outside, I'd have come in anyway. "How long will it take?"

"A few minutes." He continued clicking.

A fae shimmered to my right and slammed a witch in a blue sports coat onto the ground. Shade hurled a butter knife, but, big surprise, they weren't weighted right for throwing. It bounced off the side of the fae's head and landed on the carpet.

Mayhem threw hellfire, charring a wing, and the fae dropped his shroud to reveal his pincers opening and closing half an inch from his prey's face. Poisonous saliva dripped onto the witch's mouth.

"Help me," the man squeaked.

"Any time now, Miles." I clutched a knife, heating it as I marched toward the fae. Mayhem shot a solid stream of fire at his back, and his wings fluttered, raining bits of char onto the witch as he plunged his hand into the man's gut.

Grabbing a tuft of white hair, I yanked the fae's head up and jabbed a knife beneath his chin. It passed through his open mouth and lodged in the front of his brain, hopefully lobotomizing the bastard.

I kicked the side of his head, and he fell onto his back at Shade's feet. "He's all yours."

"I'd like to draw the life out of you slowly, but I'll make do with a knife." Shade lifted an armored plate and put an end to fae number two.

"Doors are opening," Miles said. "Go out the back and make a left down the service hall, take the second right, go through the third door on your left, and take the stairs to the basement. The vault will be on your right about twenty yards down."

"You expect me to remember all that?" I moved toward the door, still scanning the room for our invisible foes.

"What about the three other soldiers?" Shade asked.

"I'm almost done with the wards," Ash replied. "Get the amulet and get out. The other witches will have to handle them on their own."

"I don't like leaving people to die." I whirled toward Hazel, ready to drag her to safety, but she had already darted out the door.

"Imagine how many more will perish if we don't complete our quest." Mayhem gently touched my elbow, guiding me toward the back exit.

Across the room, the massive double doors swung on their hinges, opening to the foyer, and I caught a glimpse of my sister and her demon holding hands. Ash's eyes were closed as she recited an incantation.

"I will keep her safe," Chaos said in my earpiece.

"You sure as hell better." I slipped through the back door with Mayhem and Shade, yanking it closed behind me.

The sweet bliss of silence engulfed us as we made our way down the wide service hall. The speckled white linoleum felt cool on my bare feet, taming the heat of adrenaline rushing through my veins. A bead of sweat from beneath my left boob rolled down my stomach, and my heart hammered so hard in my chest, I thought it might bust through my ribs.

We turned down the second hallway, and I stopped. "Wait. Is this right, or were we supposed to take the third left?"

"You're good," Miles said. "Keep going."

"The wards are down," Ash said. "We're going in to close the rift."

"No." I turned around, ready to run to my sister's aid, but Mayhem caught me by the shoulders.

"They are capable." He pinned me with a pointed gaze. "We'll do our part. Let Ash do hers."

I ground my teeth. "It's not supposed to be her part."

"And battling fae wasn't supposed to be ours." He squeezed my shoulders and let them go. "The circumstances have changed, but the outcome must remain the same."

I wanted to argue. I really did, but once again, the

demon was right. Ash was capable. We would all do what we had to do. "Where next, Miles?"

"Third door on your left."

We followed his directions and headed downstairs to the basement, but a sickening sensation formed in my stomach as we approached the vault. A pair of black boots lay just inside the open door, and as we crept closer, I realized they weren't just boots. They were still attached to someone's feet.

"This whole thing was a setup." I swallowed the bile from the back of my throat. "The so-called security breach, locking us in the buffet room... *We* were the buffet for the fae."

I stopped outside the vault and toed the person's boot. They didn't react. With a deep inhale, I steeled myself for whatever we might find—or not find—inside and stepped around the person's legs.

A single bullet hole marred the center of the guard's head. Blood pooled beneath her, and her hands still clutched a rifle, her finger on the trigger. She never got the chance to fight back.

Mayhem strode into the vault, stepping over the dead woman, and examined the shelves. "It isn't here."

"Are you sure?" I joined him inside, though I knew he was right. We weren't simply a smorgasbord for the overgrown bugs. The fae wanted the amulet as badly as we did. They'd feasted on witch hearts and lifted the artifact in one fell swoop.

"Would they have taken it across the veil?" Shade joined us, scanning the shelves in vain.

Hazel's clicking heels preceded her appearance in the doorway, and she glanced at my bare feet. She clutched a pistol in one hand, and the amulet dangled from the golden chain entwined in her fingers. "The fae want this too?"

"As if you didn't know." I took two steps toward her, cursing myself for falling for her act. I should have trusted my intuition about her from the start.

She retreated two steps back and adjusted her grip on the pistol. "I don't know anything about those creatures. They weren't part of the plan."

Nervous tension rolled off her in waves, her gaze bouncing around the room before it landed on the dead guard. Her breath caught as she gestured at the body. "I didn't want to do that."

"What plan?" I moved toward her again, raising my hands in a show of fake innocence.

She backed out the doorway and lifted the gun, so I stopped my advance. If I'd practiced spell-casting as much as Ash had, I could freeze her without a potion, grab the amulet, and we'd be on our way. Maybe I'd have time to work on that when all this was through. For now, my choices were burning her or hurling the improperly weighted butter knife still nestled in my cleavage. Neither option sounded appealing.

"You didn't steal the amulet for the fae?" Shade moved beside me. I lifted a finger, silently telling him not to advance. Hazel was on the verge of either killing us or tucking tail and running.

Mayhem stood behind me, not saying a word, but I could feel his anger building. Maybe that was why I didn't want to hurt Hazel. Hecate knew she deserved whatever it would take for us to get the damn amulet.

I ran my finger over his mark on my arm, and he inhaled deeply, calming just enough for me to begin feeling rage.

Hazel's expression pinched. "I don't think so. The man who hired me said he was a High Priest. At first, when you asked to see it, I thought it was you. But why would you tell me to meet you in Worcester if you were coming to New York, anyway?"

"Worcester?" My eye twitched. "Did you get his name?"

She laughed. "No, but now that I know how valuable this is, I'm going to renegotiate my price. What's it do?"

"Bad things." My legs tensed, my muscles coiling, ready to spring. There were three of us and only one of her. Sure, she had a gun, but we could take her. We'd subdue her and get the amulet before she handed it over to Boston. I had no doubt Adrian was the High Priest who'd hired her.

"You can't sell it." I lunged toward her, but she slammed a heavy metal gate in my face, the lock engaging with a *thunk* as my forehead struck a bar. *Oof.*

"You have no idea what's going to happen if you do this." I reached through the grate, but she stepped farther back, tucking the gun into her waistband. "Hazel, please. We need that amulet. The fate of the world is dangling from your fingers."

She cocked her head, shrugging one shoulder. "I need the money."

I was done being nice. Mayhem and I gathered fire in our palms, ready to throw it, but before we could, she slammed the massive vault door, six *clunks* sounding as she spun the dial and locked us inside.

CHAPTER 10
EMBER

"Effing Adrian." I grasped the metal gate and shook it, not that I thought I could tear it from its hinges. Mayhem might be able to, but we'd still be stuck behind a two-foot-thick vault door with a complex, massive locking system that Ash's little lock-picking toolkit wouldn't stand a chance against.

"Effing Hazel and mother effing fae." I paced in front of the door, tripping over the dead guard and pressing my hands to my cheeks. "Shit. This poor woman."

"We have worse things to worry about." Mayhem lifted her and carried her body behind a shelving unit, out of sight.

I closed my eyes and pinched the bridge of my nose. Never did I ever dream my life would come to a point where I had worse things to worry about than a woman getting killed for being in the way of what I needed.

"Ash, Miles, are you there?" I pressed my fingers to the earpiece, but all I heard was a bit of static.

"The walls are too thick." Shade examined the gate, shaking it like I had done. "Best we can do is hope they heard us before Hazel locked us in."

"Fabulous." I lifted my hands and dropped them at my sides. "What about phones? Mayhem, hand me mine."

He fished my device from his jacket pocket and gave it to me. The words *No Service* lit up the center of the screen, so I handed it back to him.

I took a deep breath and blew it out hard. "Let's take stock. What do we know?" I made a grabby motion at Shade. "Tell me."

"Hazel has the amulet." He leaned against the gate, crossing his arms. "And she's planning to sell it to Adrian...or so we assume."

"Worcester doesn't have a coven, and it's on the way to Boston. Adrian hired her for sure." I continued pacing, keeping my body occupied so my brain could do the work. "What else?"

"She appeared to be as surprised about the fae dropping in as we were," Mayhem said.

"Right. She didn't know she was setting us up to be slaughtered. That's obvious." I grabbed the sides of my bra and hauled it up, putting my boobs back into place.

"She is a skilled actress, though," Mayhem said. "We all fell for her show of innocence."

"Did Adrian know about the fae?" Shade ignored his admission. "Or was it an unfortunate coincidence?"

"That was no coincidence." I tapped my index finger against my lips. "I think he pretended to make amends with Prince Ignacus and set up the whole thing. *We* were the peace offering."

"Ignacus promised him immeasurable power in return for his fealty. Why would he need to pretend?" Mayhem examined an antique apothecary chest, opening and closing the drawers, finding them empty.

"Ignacus lies. Adrian lies. Neither can trust their right hands to know what the left is doing. Why would Adrian turn over the amulet when he could keep all the power to himself?" I crossed my arms, shifting my weight to one leg. "He wouldn't."

"So Hazel's on her way to Worcester," Shade said. "If she makes it that far, she'll sell the amulet to Adrian. We still have two-thirds of it, so he won't get 'immeasurable' power. Just a little boost."

"A little boost like Chrys? You saw what it did to her. It changed her." I rested my hands on my hips. "Adrian is a thorn in our side now. Once he gets his hands on the amulet, and it affects his brain, he'll be an entire bramble."

"We must intercept it before Hazel initiates the exchange." Mayhem strolled toward the gate and shook it the same way Shade and I had. One corner of his mouth lifted into a smirk as he glanced sideways at me. "Back up, please."

I moved to stand next to Shade as Mayhem tightened his grip on the bars. His muscles tensed, new ones not normally visible protruding beneath his skin as he strained. He inhaled, exhaled hard, inhaled. On his next exhale, he ripped the gate from the wall and tossed it aside as if it were made of foam.

"Impressive." I couldn't fight my smile or ignore the flutter in my belly. I was in love with a strong man. So what? "Can you do that to the vault door too?"

My demon ran his fingers around the seal before bracing his palms against the center and pushing with all his might. No hinges creaked. No walls groaned against the pressure.

He leaned his shoulder against it, pushing for a few seconds before backing away and slamming his weight against the door. Nothing. "I'm afraid even my strength is no match for this."

"What if we all tried together?" Shade braced his arm, angling his shoulder toward the door. "On three."

He counted. We shoved. Twice. Three times. Nothing moved.

I gripped my aching shoulder, rotating it to loosen the tension. "When brawn doesn't work, we have to use our brains. Fabulous."

"We are surrounded by magical artifacts." Mayhem leaned down to kiss the bruise already forming on my shoulder. "Surely you can find something of use."

I spun in a circle, taking in the possibilities. "Except we don't know if these things actually do what the tags say they do. They were wrong about the amulet."

I lifted the information sheet. "'A nineteen-carat Burma ruby, rumored to increase physical strength tenfold.' They had no idea."

"How could they?" Mayhem picked up a gem-encrusted dagger, the blade intricately etched with Celtic designs. "The amulet was never meant to see this side of the veil. Discord should have left it in Hell when Isabel summoned us."

"Our lives would be a helluva lot easier if he had." I tossed the info sheet into the black velvet box where the answer to—and cause of—our problems should have lain. "I wonder who listed it, and why they'd want to sell it."

"If the bearer lacked a strong inborn ability such as fire or another element, the amulet's power would be difficult to ascertain."

"You have to have power to increase power," Shade said.

"Precisely. Which is why your friend Chrys was able to harness it fully. She was a force." He said it matter-of-factly, and I knew deep down he was *my* demon and what experiences he'd had before we got together didn't matter.

But he'd been inside Chrys the same way Chaos had been inside Ash. The way he'd been inside me for a short time. Jealousy reared its ugly head again, but I squelched it. Mayhem was mine. Period. End of story.

He handed me the gem-encrusted dagger. "Perhaps this could be of use."

"It's beautiful." I accepted the weapon, but the moment my skin touched the blue and green stones on the handle, sparks ignited on my fingers. "Son of a bitch." I dropped it, letting it clatter on the floor as I wiped my hand on my dress.

The sparks hadn't just ignited on my hand; it had felt like the dagger was drawing my fire out. "What does the info sheet say?"

"I didn't check." Mayhem handed it to me and picked up the dagger, turning it over in his hands.

"It's a vessel." I read and re-read the description. "It can hold magic and release it later. A spell or an inborn power. Let me see it."

I held out my hand and focused on keeping my

magic inside me. This time, it didn't pull my power from my skin. "I wonder…"

Focusing my intent, I let fire build in the core of my being and sent it down my arm, into the dagger. The blade glowed deep red as I filled it, and when I'd given it all it would hold, the metal faded to its normal hue.

"See if you can release the fire." I offered the handle to Shade. "But keep your own magic inside you."

He accepted the weapon and examined the blade before pointing it at the floor. "Is there a trigger or something I need to say?"

I flipped the info sheet over, but the back was blank. "It doesn't say. Maybe it just needs your intent."

He lifted the blade and thrust it toward the floor. Fire—*my* fire—shot from the tip to billow on the tile. I called to it, drawing it back inside as if I'd been the one to shoot the flames.

"That's cool." Shade arched a brow and studied the gems on the handle. "It's not going to open the door, but it could definitely come in handy later."

I took the dagger and returned it to its velvet box. "We need to focus and find something that can help us with an unlocking spell."

We scoured the shelves, reading the info cards and examining the artifacts, my stomach sinking further and further. I could think of sinister uses for nearly every item in the room, especially a dagger that could steal power from an unsuspecting witch.

We could murder, maim, and drive people mad with the stuff in the vault. Sadly, we couldn't find a single item to help us walk through walls or magically pick a lock.

"There's nothing." My sinking stomach twisted, pulling my heart down with it. My insides tightened, my heart hammering so hard, I could see each rapid beat in my chest. I took a deep breath, trying to stave off my anxiety.

Panicking at this disco wouldn't do us any good, but my body ignored my brain's command to chill the eff out. My palms slicked with sweat, and my mouth went dry. "What are we going to do?"

Mayhem took both my hands and kissed the backs of my fingers. "You must cast an unlocking spell without a potion. You are strong enough."

I laughed dryly. "Even if I could, I'd need access to the witchy web to look up an incantation. I don't know one off the top of my head."

"I do." Shade set a wooden box onto a shelf and cast his gaze to the floor before meeting my eyes. "I remember the one I used to break into your house."

I crossed my arms. "Ah, yes. Good times."

Mayhem gave me a questioning look, and I shrugged. "Long story. He's forgiven." I returned my attention to Shade. "Did you cast it without a potion?"

His jaw tightened. "No. It was a complex spell."

"Which you only had to use on a couple of dead-bolts." I gestured to the circular vault door. "Do you really think it'll work on that?"

Shade straightened, his knee-jerk egotistical reaction simmering just below the surface before his shoulders slumped. "Not without a potion, no."

"It must." Grasping my hand, Mayhem led me toward the door. "We have no other options."

Shade sauntered toward us and stood on Mayhem's other side. "It's worth a shot. I have no intention of dying in here."

I ground my teeth. "Spellcasting has never been my strength. Ash..."

"Is not here." Mayhem squeezed my hand. "Spell-casting is not your strength because you prefer to fight. That doesn't mean it's your weakness. You can do this."

"We'll do it together." Shade held his hand toward my demon, and Mayhem accepted it. "The incantation is easy, but your focus has to be intense." He recited the words he'd memorized.

I swallowed the dryness from my mouth. Two sentences. That's all it was. Two simple sentences that we had to infuse with so much power, our vim would dwindle to nothing when we were through.

And even then, the spell might not work.

No, I couldn't think that way. I refused to manifest

our demise with negativity. Ash needed me. Cinder needed me. Salem...hell, the world...needed me—us—to break the curse, mend the veil, and set things right again.

"Let's do it." I tightened my grip on Mayhem and rested my free hand against the circular door. Setting my intention, I said a silent prayer to the goddess and gathered my vim into the core of my being. *Hecate, please don't forsake us.*

My power built, growing hotter, stronger inside me, and the energy in the room shifted with my magic. Pressure formed around us, squeezing and filling the room with buzzing electricity. Shade rested his hand against the door, and Mayhem opened to us.

Demonic energy surged through my veins, my entire body electrifying with pinpricks and dark magic. I reveled in it, rolling the sensation over and over in my mind, my soul. It no longer felt foreign inside me. Mayhem's power felt as much a part of me as my own.

"Ready?" I asked.

Shade gasped before clearing his throat. "Yeah."

"Lock engaged, hear my page. Open now; my passing you'll allow," we said in unison., and I swear I heard electricity crackling around us.

We repeated the spell a second time. Then a third. The buzzing increased, Mayhem's low vibration mixing and melding with Shade's and my high. I willed the magic outward through my palm, but the lock didn't budge. I focused, listening for the gears turning in the door. Not even an infinitesimal sound indicated the spell was working.

Because it wasn't working.

Not yet.

"Give us more," I said, and Mayhem released another surge of magic. It crashed into my psyche, making me sway on my feet.

"Too much," Shade ground out, but I couldn't get enough.

"Come over here. I'll filter it." I reached for Shade, and he dropped my demon's hand.

His breath came out in a rush, and he stumbled, catching himself on the door. "I can't."

"You can. Don't give up." I took his hand and tugged him to my side. "Touch the door."

He did as I asked, and I sent a tiny amount of Mayhem into Shade. "You okay?"

"Yeah." He raked in a breath. "I'm ready."

Mayhem gave me more, no longer having to divide it between us, and I let the power trickle into Shade's palm. We recited the incantation again, and the door groaned.

Adrenaline surged through me, spiraling around Mayhem's magic, merging and intensifying the sensations as we spoke the words a second time.

Shade panted before heaving in a breath, his body

trembling with the magical exertion. We recited the spell again, and my head spun. Darkness closed in, my vision tunneling, stars swimming in front of me.

I pushed out as much magic as I could, focusing my intent on the massive lock inside the door. Sharp pain sliced from my jaw to my temple. I strained. Shade wheezed. The door groaned.

"One more push," I said as if we were giving birth to a ten-pound magical baby.

The lock clunked once. Twice. Six times.

Shade tugged from my grasp and slumped against the door. Mayhem pulled his magic back, leaving me empty, my vim depleted to nothingness. My tunneling vision went black.

CHAPTER II
EMBER

Sunlight streaming in through the window turned the backs of my eyelids red. I kept them closed, willing myself to slip back under, into the deep sleep the morning had dragged me out of. The pillow, so indulgent it had to be made of down, cradled my head as I snuggled into the softest sheets I'd ever felt.

Mayhem lay beside me, his arm draped across my stomach, the heat of his body adding to my blissful comfort. I opened my eyes, turning my head toward him and smiling at the sight of him sleeping peacefully.

So this was what it felt like to wake up next to your soulmate. My chest warmed, squeezing my heart in a way that felt simultaneously euphoric and painful. I rolled to my side to face him, and he stirred, snorting gently before his eyes opened, his gaze meeting mine.

"Good morning." I caressed his face, running my thumb across his cheek.

He sucked in a quick breath and rose onto his elbow. "It isn't morning. I didn't mean to fall asleep." He pushed to sit upright. "How are you feeling? Is the headache gone?"

"Headache?" I furrowed my brow. "I feel fine. Actually, I feel great. Lay back down with me."

He rested his palm on my forehead, his posture relaxing with his exhale. "Thank Lucifer. The fever is gone."

"What fever? I'm fine." I rose onto my elbow and took in my surroundings for the first time. Massive windows provided an amazing view of the bustling city below, and plush, beige carpet covered the floor. My bedroom floor was hardwood, and I didn't own anything made of down. We weren't at home, snuggled into my bed like I'd thought. I scrunched my brow, trying to put the pieces of this puzzling scenario together.

"I'm confused." I sat up fully and ran my hand down the little black dress I wore. I'd slept in my clothes? Well, most of them. "Where's my bra?"

"You complained about the garment multiple times, so I removed it when I laid you down. You are fully recovered?"

"Recovered from what? I can't remember how I got here. Are we in the penthouse? What time is it?"

"Indeed, we are. It's just past two in the afternoon." He brushed his fingers to my forehead, smoothing an errant strand of hair into place. "What is the last thing you remember?"

"Two? I slept all day?" I scratched my head, my fingers getting caught on a knot of tangled hair. "I don't... The amulet. We stole the amulet."

He smiled sadly. "We tried. The shadow witch Hazel took it and locked us in the vault. Do you remember that?"

"I don't." I worried my bottom lip between my teeth, racking my brain for the memories. "I remember Hazel. She was so hot for you, I nearly strangled her, but I..."

The memories came flooding back. She'd let Shade in, and then there was the security breach. And the rift. And... "The fae. Ash! Is she okay?"

"Your sister is fine. She and Chaos helped the others fight. She sealed the rift, and Chaos used his magic to make them forget what had happened."

"Thank the goddess. And Shade and Miles? Are they?"

"Miles is attending to Shade as he recovers. Hopefully, he'll wake up soon so we can be on our way."

"Recovers from what? Why can't I remember?"

"You and Shade cast an unlocking spell that drained you both. You passed out as the vault door opened, and we carried you here so you could rest comfortably."

"Oh. Oh!" His description finally jogged the rest of the missing memories into view. "Hazel is selling it to Adrian. We have to stop her."

I untangled myself from the covers and stood on the floor. My head spun, and I sat on the edge of the bed. "That was one helluva spell."

"You also channeled more of my magic than you ever have before. It's no wonder you slept so long." He sat next to me. "The power I gave you would have killed anyone else. You truly are the most amazing woman I have ever met."

I rested my hand on his thigh, my heart warming at his words. "I'm your soulmate. You have to say that."

He grasped my hand, bringing it to his lips and kissing the backs of my fingers. "I love hearing you say that. I love you, Ember."

"I know." My stomach did flip-flops as he held my gaze. "I love you too."

A giggle bubbled up from my chest, and I pressed my lips together, cutting it off short. "I love you too."

He inhaled deeply, the purple in his irises turning fluid before he leaned in and kissed me. The softness of his lips made me shiver, the slow, purposeful movements of his tongue against mine making me forget the rest of the world existed.

I could have stayed in that moment forever, feeling him, drinking him in, relishing his love. But my brain, ever the strategic bitch, wouldn't shut up about our next steps. I broke the kiss, pulling back to gaze into his eyes.

"We have to go to Worcester. Good goddess, she could have already made the exchange. I need to scry for her. For the amulet." I stood, and thankfully the room didn't tip on its side.

"Your sister and Chaos are following her. They borrowed a car from a rental place."

"Borrowed." I laughed dryly, my gaze locking on the jewel-encrusted dagger lying on the nightstand. "I suppose you borrowed that too?"

"Oh, I have no intention of returning it. Consider it an early wedding present."

Wedding. The word on his lips made my insides twist into knots. None of us would get to experience the elusive happily ever after fate wanted us to believe we would have. There would be no weddings. No settling down, no starting families. Nothing.

So, stop thinking about it, Em. I pushed the thoughts from my mind.

"Thank you." It was all I could think to mutter. Truth be told, I'd considered stealing the dagger too... before I'd blacked out.

Gah! I'd wasted so much time sleeping. We needed to get moving, but... "I'm starving. Do we have any food?"

"I will order room service while you get dressed. When Shade recovers, we will take the van to Worcester to meet Chaos and Ash."

"Sounds like a plan. I'm going to take a quick shower." I licked my lips, remembering the last shower I'd taken. When Mayhem had taken me.

"As much as I would love to join you," he said as if reading my mind, "we are on a schedule. I'm afraid I would keep you here all day if we became intimate now."

I'd be lying if I said I wasn't disappointed, but he was right. He'd keep me there all day, and I would enjoy every second of it. "Will you order me a burger with extra fries? And the biggest Coke they have."

"Of course." He smiled and strode out of the room.

I tossed my dress and underwear onto a chair and padded to the bathroom, cringing at my reflection in the mirror. My mascara had run, giving me raccoon eyes, and my hair looked like a squirrel had nested on my head again. Lovely.

I showered, using the expensive hotel conditioner to work the tangles out of my hair, and dressed in my normal fireproof black pants and shirt. After putting on my boots, I strode into the living room to find all three guys sitting at the table.

"How are you?" I asked Shade as I sank into a chair next to my demon.

"Better now. That's the most comfortable bed I've ever slept in."

"I know, right? I forgot where I was and that the rest of the world existed when I woke up this morn... this afternoon."

"Room service," a woman called over the intercom.

"Come in." Miles pressed the button, and she pushed in a cart draped in white linen, with four plates covered in silver domes. He gave her a tip, and she went on her way.

I devoured my burger before moving on to the mountain of thick-cut fries and washing it all down with a quart of Coke. The guys did the same, and we gathered our gear to load the van. Mayhem hit the button for the elevator, and I cast a longing glance at the penthouse.

"One day, we'll stay in a place like this on vacation," I said. "No beasties to fight. No mysteries to solve. No artifacts to steal."

"No veil to mend," Shade added.

I sighed, trying to ignore the way my heart wrenched at his words. That was the one part I was not looking forward to. There had to be a way to mend the veil with the demons on this side. How could I live if there wasn't?

People cast us strange glances as we filed out of

the lobby, which was fair. Dressed in all black and carrying duffel bags rather than designer suitcases, we certainly didn't look like their normal clientele.

A sense of calm washed over me as I climbed into the driver's seat and started the engine. This van was one thing I could manage while my life spiraled out of control. I could turn the wheel and press the pedals and take my team to the roadside motel in Worcester, where my sister and her demon had set up to spy on Hazel.

According to Ash's texts, Adrian, or whoever would be his delegate, hadn't arrived to claim the amulet. With any luck, we'd be there before the exchange went down. Hazel would be lucky if we were. I doubted Adrian planned to pay her a penny.

Most likely, she'd pay him with her life.

CHAPTER 12
MAYHEM

It took three and a half earthly hours to reach the town they called Worcester. The sun sank behind the horizon, painting the sky in shades of deep orange and purple before it disappeared, making way for the moon to reflect its light in silver hues.

The motel in which Chaos and Ash had spent the night resembled a dumpster compared to our New York penthouse, but they assured us Hazel resided in the room next door. Ember parked the van on the opposite end of the building, out of sight from the main road...and Hazel's view. Miles and Shade placed a ward on the vehicle, and we gathered weapons before creeping quietly to room one-twenty-seven.

Two beds, each barely large enough to sleep a single demon, took up most of the space, and a minuscule round table with two stained chairs sat near the shaded window. Ash spoke, though she emitted no sound. In fact, even the heated air blowing from the vent created no audible vibrations.

Ash waved her hand, and my ears popped, her voice becoming clear. "I brought you into the silencing spell so you can speak freely. I also put an amplifier on her room so we can hear her better."

"She hasn't left since we arrived," Chaos said. "She had food delivered once, and she talks on the phone to a friend in New York."

"Any idea why Adrian's making her wait?" Ember curled her lip at the untouched bed and took off the thin, brown covering before sinking onto the edge of the mattress.

"We're not even sure he's the one she's meeting," Ash said. "She's spoken to both a man and a woman about it, but we'll find out soon enough. It's going down in half an hour."

"I'm glad we made it in time." I sat next to Ember, and the mattress squeaked as it absorbed my weight. A red ring stained the faux-wood nightstand, and one side of the drawer handle hung loose. "I'm also glad we won't have to stay the night in these sub-par accommodations."

"You spent four centuries in prison, and you're worried about sleeping in a seedy motel?" Ember adjusted her position, curling her lip as the mattress springs groaned. "Can't say I blame you."

"Any minute now." Hazel's voice sounded as if she were in the room with us. "You know how melodramatic High Priests can be. He probably wants to meet there for the aesthetic."

I gave my brother a questioning look. "Adrian isn't coming here?"

"He wishes to meet her in the cemetery across the street," Chaos said.

"That tracks." Shade laughed dryly and sank into a chair. "She's not wrong about the melodrama. Remember his throne?"

"Why are we waiting for Adrian to arrive?" I asked. "Could we not break down her door and take the amulet now, saving all of us the trouble of dealing with the High Priest again?"

"Good question." Ember patted my thigh. "Why are we just sitting here?"

"She doesn't have it on her person," Chaos said.

"She hid it somewhere before she got here." Ash rose and padded to a sink at the back of the room. "Apparently, she wore it on the drive over and it's already affected her. She's been bragging to her friend about how strong the wards she put on the amulet and her room are."

An array of bottles sat on the counter, and Ash arranged them in her bag. "I tried scrying for it, but she hid it well. We'll have to follow her when she leaves and wait for her to uncover it. Shade can cloak us."

"She can see through my shadows." Shade drummed his fingers on the table. "Can't you mind control her and make her hand it over?"

"We tried that too," Ash said. "The wards she set up are stronger than anything I've experienced. If she hadn't checked in under her real name, we'd never have found her."

"Yet you were able to amplify the sounds of her warded room..." I arched a brow.

"The amulet made her stronger, not smarter." Ash shrugged. "She's not letting anything in, but she didn't bother herself with noise getting out."

"As far as she knows, we're still locked in the vault." Ember rose, turning left and right, but there was no room for her to pace. She sat back down. "She's got dollar signs in her eyes. I doubt she considered someone might try to intercept it."

"What about her?" Hazel's voice drifted through the wall. "Unless she can conjure four times what she offered, she's not a player in this game. The High Priest offered me twenty grand."

Ember's brows crept toward her hairline. "She has multiple prospects?"

"That explains why she's been negotiating with a

man and a woman," Ash said. "I didn't make the connection that it could be two different buyers."

"I'm going to demand forty," Hazel said. "Because, Mom, with forty, we can keep the house."

We remained silent, waiting for her to speak again.

"I'd like to see them try," she continued. "It made me so strong. You'll see. I'll be home tonight with *fifty* grand in my pocket and more power than all our ancestors combined. I have to go… Yes, I'll be careful. Blessed be."

Hazel's lock disengaged. The door opened and closed. Miles pulled back the curtain slightly, watching her as she exited the motel. "She's heading to the cemetery on foot. Maybe she hid the amulet there."

Ember rose and stretched the tension from her neck. "Here's the plan. Shade, you'll cloak us. Like you said, seeing through shadow is active magic. She's so distracted with the thought of money, she might not use her power."

"And if she does?" Chaos asked.

"We'll do our best to stay out of sight." She slipped past me and stood at the foot of the bed. "Ash, can you make our bubble of silence mobile?"

"I can do that."

"She is away from her ward of protection." I stood and moved toward the door. "We could grab her now. Put her out of her misery if she refuses to cooperate."

My witch held up a finger. "Everyone is keeping their misery intact. Understood? No more dead bodies."

I spread my hands, conceding. "I understand, though she did attempt to kill us. You would have suffocated slowly had you not mastered the unlocking spell."

"She's in the cemetery." Miles let the curtain fall into place.

Ember clutched our stolen dagger, filling it with fire magic before handing it to Shade. "Just in case."

"I don't…" He started to protest but clamped his mouth shut and accepted the weapon, also accepting his magical limitations. He was the only one of us who could not throw magic at a distance.

"Let's head out. The moment she grabs the amulet, we move in." Ember turned to me. "Subdue her, but do *not* kill her."

If anyone else spoke to me in this manner, I would make a point to kill Hazel the moment I saw her. But Ember wasn't anyone else. She was *my* witch, and I would gladly obey her every command.

Or do my best to obey. I could make no guarantees.

We filed out of our tiny room, and though Shade's cloak turned the world gray around us, we kept to the shadows. Our team remained silent, the weight of the task at hand settling on our shoulders, the fate of this world a heavy burden on our backs.

How easy it would be to grab Ember and whisk her to the Underworld, ridding ourselves of the encumbrance. A witch of her power would survive the transition. Her sister had proven that. She would technically be dead when she reached Hell, therefore unable to return to this realm.

But she would be mine for eternity.

Though, if I took her against her will, she would be certain to make eternity a *living hell* for us both. I chuckled, wondering how Discord was fairing with Cinder. If she were half as feisty as her sisters, he would no doubt be suffering.

"Something funny?" Ember asked, drawing me from my rumination. We had crossed the street and now gathered behind a mausoleum, out of Hazel's line of vision. She peeked past the wall, pressing her fingertips to the stone.

"Not at all," I said, my thoughts turning to darkness. Their plan to mend the veil involved bringing Cinder back from the dead. They couldn't possibly understand the consequences of such an act. Without Lucifer's blessing, the feat would be nearly impossible, and even with his approval, necromancy was dark magic. They had already cast a phoenix spell to bring me back. What would performing the darkest of dark magic do to their vim...their souls?

"Your sister—" I began.

"Shit. Adrian's here with his posse." Ember ducked

behind the mausoleum, leaning her back against the white stucco wall. I could see her heart pounding against her chest.

"There's something—" I tried again to discuss the issue we'd have with Cinder, but she cut me off, holding up a finger.

"Shh. Listen." She leaned her head against the wall and closed her eyes.

"Where's the amulet?" Adrian asked, his voice grating on my nerves the same way it had when we'd encountered him last.

"Where's my money?" Hazel answered with a question of her own.

I moved in front of Ember, the urge to pull her into my arms, open a rift, and run to Hell so strong, I nearly did just that. Instead, I leaned to my left, peering around the building to witness the attempted exchange.

The same witches we had encountered before fanned out around Adrian as he scoffed. "Gray, who's with her?"

His shadow witch narrowed her eyes, and I stepped back, out of view. "She's alone as far I can see, but..."

I waited a beat or two for Gray to finish—she no doubt had qualms about Hazel's strength since she had the amulet in her possession—but she trailed off, leaving her opinion unspoken.

"We'll wire you the money when you hand over the amulet," Adrian said. "Where is it?"

I peered around the mausoleum again. Hazel had her back to us, and Gray no longer squinted, so I stepped closer to get a better view.

"Mayhem!" Ember whisper shouted, though Ash's silencing spell still held strong.

"I'm not an idiot." Hazel crossed her arms. "Set up the wire. Show me you have fifty K ready to send me, and then I'll get the amulet."

The High Priest laughed, the noise sounding like it belonged to an exaggerated movie villain. "Our agreement was twenty."

She shrugged one shoulder dismissively. "I have another buyer lined up if you don't want it."

"Who?" Adrian asked. "Are they from Salem? I highly doubt they have the funds available to beat my offer."

"The Salem witches tried to steal it." Hazel shifted her weight to one leg, resting her hand on her hip. "I left them in the vault in New York."

Ember tensed beside me, her energy shifting into fight mode. Good. I would love to tear Adrian's head from his neck. Perhaps I could use it as a bowling ball in the Underworld. The Severed Heads League had invited me to join their ranks before Isabel imprisoned me.

"Does she have it yet?" my witch asked through clenched teeth.

"She has not revealed its location," I said.

Chaos moved beside me, his expression grim. "Do you feel it? Focus on the veil."

I shifted my attention from the imbecile witches playing with a force they could never fully comprehend to the energy around us. The low vibration of the Underworld registered immediately, making my arm hairs stand on end.

"A rift is forming." I scanned our surroundings but found no visual clues. Not yet. "Wait. There are two."

"I feel them both as well," Chaos said. "Ready yourselves for company. We aren't the only ones preparing to intercept the amulet."

Ember unsheathed her sword while Miles and Shade clutched daggers in each hand. Ash rubbed her thumbs against her fingertips, making them spark before adjusting the strap of her bag.

"Bring it on," Ember said.

"One rift is there." I pointed to the shimmering line of red forming three feet away. It hadn't yet opened, but the energy from the being wishing to cross over was palpable.

"Let's seal it before anything gets through." Ember gripped her sword in one hand and offered the other Ash. They spoke the incantation, and Ash dusted the tear with her potion. The red line faded, closing before it could fully open.

Adrian laughed again, drawing my attention to the exchange. "Did one of them have purple hair? And one with blue?"

"Purple, yes. A woman with two men. I didn't see anyone with blue."

He laughed harder. "You locked the High Priestess of Salem in a vault. I suppose I can give you a bonus for getting her out of my hair." He snapped his fingers at a male witch. "Hector, pull up the wire transfer and change the amount to thirty thousand."

"I want fifty or I'll take it to the other buyer."

Adrian arched a brow. "You'll take thirty and hand it over...if you value your life."

Hazel shifted her weight from foot to foot, crossing and uncrossing her arms. "Forty-five."

Adrian inclined his chin, tilting his head in warning.

Hazel's posture deflated. "Okay. Thirty. Show it to me."

Adrian jerked his head toward her, and Hector showed her a phone. I was too far away to see the contents of the screen, but Hazel nodded and stepped away.

"It's a deal," she said.

"It's about damn time." Ember stepped around the

wall to stand next to me. "You said two rifts were forming. Where's the other one?"

I focused on the vibrations in the air. "Behind Adrian. I believe it's from the fae realm."

"I agree," Chaos said. "The question is, did Adrian invite them?"

"Doesn't matter." Ember clutched her sword with both hands. "We're here for the amulet. Let Boston deal with their own problems."

A blast of power shot through the rift, blinding light enveloping us, the force of the wind so strong, Adrian and his witches stumbled. Three fae soldiers entered our realm, the first latching onto Hector so quickly he didn't have time to gasp before the creature plunged his talons into the witch's chest and ripped out his still-beating heart.

CHAPTER 13

EMBER

"Well, that escalated quickly." I crept toward Hazel, planning to drag her away from the fray and force her to give us the amulet, but another, bigger fae crawled through the massive rift.

This one had glistening wings like a dragonfly and round, faceted, silver eyes protruding from his forehead. An array of stone-like extensions circled his skull, or the top of his exoskeleton head, or...whatever these buggy bastards had...in the shape of a built-in crown, and soldier number one lowered to one knee, holding the heart up like an offering to the big guy.

Adrian dropped to his knee like the follower he was, and his minions cowered behind him while poor Hector lay heartless—and liverless—at the fae's feet.

"Ignacus," Mayhem growled beside me, his lip

curling in disgust before he sucked in a sharp breath. "Another rift is forming."

"Adrian said they weren't planning an invasion here." Ash clutched a potion bottle in one hand and held a ball of fire in the other.

"Adrian lies." I crept a little closer. "They all do. Is our silencing spell still intact?"

"For now. Want me to reinforce it?"

I shook my head. "Take Shade and Miles around the mausoleum and get behind them. Seal the rift before any more fae get through."

"My shadow won't reach that far," Shade said. "I won't be able to cloak you."

"Same goes for the silencing," Ash said.

"That's okay. Things are about to get messy, anyway." I jerked my head, urging them to go, and turned my attention back to the display before us.

Adrian, still kneeling in faux deference, held one hand behind his back and twirled his finger, quietly gathering the air toward him and answering our question. No, the cocky High Priest did not call the bug men to this little shindig.

Ignacus, the half-blooded fae prince, accepted the offered heart, opening his wide mouth and revealing a set of dagger-like teeth. Gooey saliva strings stretched from the top row to the bottom, making my stomach sour, and I tilted my head, scrunching my brow.

How could this guy be a prince and look so much

like the lesser fae we unaffectionately called over-grown mosquitoes? Wait... Did the fae king get it on with a...?

That would be like a Great Dane going for a Chihuahua. Ew. I shook away the thought.

A squelching, chomping sound drew my attention back to the moment, right in time for me to watch Ignacus devour Hector's heart and move on to his liver.

He made a clicking sound in his throat and wiped the blood from his face with a clawed hand, completely missing the dribble running down his chin. "What happened to our deal?" He straightened his spine and inclined his head, looking both regal and ridiculous at once.

No, not his spine. I kept forgetting these guys wore their skeletons on the outside. *So gross.*

Adrian looked up at Ignacus. "It's still on. I came to get the amulet, and I was planning to give it to you."

"That was not the deal." He wrapped his long, spindly fingers around Adrian's neck and hauled him to his feet. "You were to find the amulet and send word of its location."

Adrian fisted his hand, ending his call on the wind. "I did. The auction," he squeaked. "I gave you all those witches. The amulet was there."

Hazel took a tentative step backward. I clung to the edge of the mausoleum, doing my best not to draw attention. Olga looked at Hazel and gave her head a tiny shake before her gaze locked on me. Her eyes widened, her mouth dropping open with her gasp.

I pressed a finger to my lips, shushing her, and crept forward a little more. So far, the fae were focused on Adrian and his minions. If I could just grab Hazel...

Ignacus growled. "You gave us witches who knew our weak spots. Your blue-haired woman shouted orders to the rest. They slaughtered my men. Only one got away before she sealed the rift."

"That wasn't my work." Adrian swirled his finger again, finally realizing his lies and excuses weren't going to save him. "The blue-haired one is from Salem. They're your enemies, not us."

"A witch is a witch. Where is the one you sent to take my amulet?"

"Shit." Hazel turned to run, but Olga hit her with a binding spell, stopping her mid-stride.

"Apprehend her," Ignacus shouted at his soldiers, who turned on their glamour, becoming nearly invisible in the dark night.

Adrian raised his hand and slammed a gust of wind against Ignacus's head. The fae stumbled, losing his grip and allowing Adrian to jerk away and dart behind Olga and Gray.

A shimmer appeared in front of Hazel before a soldier grabbed her and dragged her toward his leader. I hurled a fireball at the culpable fae. Mayhem threw one a split second later, and the soldier dropped his camouflage.

His pincers opened and closed, poisonous goo dripping from them as he dropped Hazel and lunged for me. I sidestepped, smacking his back with my sword and letting him plow past me, into my demon. Mayhem caught him by the throat, and Chaos plunged a taloned hand beneath a breastplate, ripping out the creature's heart.

"One down, three to go." I sheathed my sword and clutched Hazel's arm, hauling her upright. Mayhem grabbed her around the waist and carried her behind the mausoleum while Chaos charged into the fray.

"I'm going to unfreeze you." I gripped her shoulders, pressing her against the wall. "And then you're going to tell me where you hid the amulet. If anyone else gets their hands on it, life as you know it will end. I'm talking catastrophic consequences. Do you understand?"

Hazel's eyes, the only part of her body she could move, darted back and forth. Why had I wasted my breath? If Olga's binding spell worked like ours, Hazel wouldn't remember a word I just said.

"The rift is sealed," Ash shouted, "but there's a new one with another beastie trying to get through."

"Go help them," I said to Mayhem.

"But the amulet—"

"I'll take care of it. Go."

He raised his hands, giving me a weird look before shaking his head and joining the others in the battle.

"What was done is now undone. Break this bind and restore her mind." I tightened my grip on Hazel's shoulders, leaning all my weight against her as I repeated my warning. "Tell me where the amulet is so I can save the world."

The witch had the audacity to laugh in my face. "Unless you've got sixty grand in your pocket, you can screw yourself."

"What part of the world ending don't you understand?" Now would be the perfect time for Ash's mind control thing she and Chaos did. Could Mayhem and I do it...? It didn't matter because I had sent him away, dammit.

Hazel laughed again. "I have problems of my own to deal with. The amulet is mine. I'll find another buyer."

"The hell you will." I sent a wave of heat down my arms and out my palms. I didn't burn her shoulders. Not yet, but I would if I had to. It wasn't very light witch-like, I knew. But *it's for the greater good* had become my excuse for doing anything unsavory lately.

"Get your hands off me." She narrowed her eyes.

"Not until you tell me where you hid the amulet." I turned up the temperature to a slow roast.

"That's not happening." She wove her hands upward, between my arms, and grabbed the back of my neck, pulling me forward with otherworldly strength while simultaneously kneeing me in the gut.

I swear my stomach nearly shredded on my spine and came out my back. The ridiculous thought of *how the hell did she get so strong* flashed through my mind, but I knew the answer. She'd worn the amulet for three hours. Of course she was strong.

Hazel shoved me into the wall, my head hitting the stone with a *thwack*, and sprinted toward another tomb. I gave chase and tackled her, but she wiggled free and kicked me in the shoulder, dislocating it with a *pop*.

I ground my teeth, groaning, a slew of cuss words flying from my lips as she dove into a mausoleum. Stumbling to my feet, I clutched my useless left arm, holding it against my body.

Shouts, grunts, and more cuss words sounded to my right. I spun toward my team. Ash kneeled next to Gray, smearing a salve on her injured neck, while Chaos knocked a soldier off his feet. Mayhem charged toward Ignacus, but effing Adrian sent a tornado for my demon, knocking him backward before he could reach the prince.

Miles hurled an energy ball at the second soldier, making him stumble, and Shade raised a hand toward the creature, attempting to suck the life from his body. I glimpsed the back of Olga's head as she high-tailed it out of the cemetery, and a massive beak protruded from a rift, followed by a feathery head with enormous golden eyes.

"Please tell me that's not another chicken-snake." I took two steps toward Hazel's mausoleum when Ignacus let out a screech, the sound so loud, it hit me in the chest, knocking me—and everyone else—to the ground.

Hazel grunted behind me. I pushed myself to sitting and turned toward her. The amulet dangled from her fingers as she clambered to her feet. "Holy shit. Is that a griffin?"

I followed her gaze to the beastie, which was definitely not a chicken-snake. This creature had the head of an eagle and the body of the biggest lion I had ever seen. It shrieked and stomped its murder mittens, making Hazel freeze in her tracks.

My instincts turned to fight, and I shot to my feet, unsheathing my sword with my good arm. The griffin prowled toward us. Hazel whimpered. I sent fire licking up my blade and swung. The griffin took to the sky.

Did I mention the beastie had huge, feathered wings?

I had never seen a griffin in real life, and apparently, neither had my team. We all stood there dumbfounded for a second, and that second was all our foe needed to gain the upper hand.

A soldier grabbed Shade by the throat and Miles by

the hair. Ignacus lunged for Chaos, tackling him to the ground while the other soldier knocked Ash onto her back, pinning her to the dirt and dripping poisonous saliva onto her face.

Adrian narrowed his eyes at Hazel and lifted his hands, creating a cyclone of grave dirt around her. She coughed and gasped, scratching at her neck as her supposed buyer sucked the air from her lungs.

Panic made my blood run cold. I used to say I could kick anyone's ass with both hands tied behind my back, but now, with one arm dangling like a limp yogurt slinger, I knew what a crock that was. I couldn't save them all...couldn't save any of them unless I acted, but for possibly the first time in my life, out of the three Fs, my body chose to effing freeze.

I stood there impotent, useless, watching... No, not even watching. My mind all but blanked while everyone around me hung on the precipice of death.

"Ember." Mayhem's voice shattered the ice, and my mind kicked into overdrive.

I lunged at him, grasping his hand. "Use me. Use my energy and make the violence stop."

"I can't stop violence, my love. I cause it."

"Not with me, you don't." I focused on the sigil warming my injured arm and pushed my magic into him.

He sucked in a breath and closed his eyes, but now was not the time for him to bask in my essence.

I squeezed his hand. "Send it out. Stop them before anyone else dies."

"Mmm...yes." He opened his eyes and shared his energy with me, drawing more of mine into him and causing the air around us to thicken. Our magic mixed and melded, and as he sent it outward, I gasped. Every nerve in my body fired at once, electrifying me, heightening my senses, sharpening my vision until I could see the griffin in the sky as clearly as if it were on the ground.

The fighting stopped. The fae soldiers backed away from my team, smacking into each other and looking confused as all get out. Adrian blinked at me, cocking his head, and Ignacus rose, offering Chaos a hand up.

Hazel sucked in a massive breath and dropped to her knees, the amulet falling from her grasp. Both Adrian and Ignacus lunged toward it. I would have done the same if I weren't busy keeping everyone from killing each other, but it wouldn't have mattered if I'd tried.

The griffin swooped from the sky, half-screeching, half-roaring, and snatched the amulet from the dirt before flying off, into the horizon. My mouth hung open as I watched it ascend and head toward the distant mountains.

"Well, what now?" Shade asked, drawing my attention to our current issue, which involved three teams ready to murder each other at the first crack of our magic.

"We will leave peacefully." Ignacus bowed slightly. "My soldiers require enzymes to remain in this realm, but we will not take them from you." He waved an arm, slicing into the fabric of reality and opening a rift to the fae world. "We will obtain the amulet another time. Do not doubt it."

The two fly-men stood at attention as their prince slipped through the veil. When they followed, the rift slammed shut, stitching itself back together. The air around us shimmied. No, not the air.

The veil.

It was as if a wall existed on every plane, like I could reach out in any direction and touch it. It was everywhere and nowhere at the same time, and my brain could not comprehend the ethereal geometry.

Squeezing my eyes shut, I shook my head before blinking them open again. Mayhem's magic still flowed through me. Adrian stood there looking as dumbfounded as I felt, and Hazel made the most of our inaction, doing an about-face and sprinting out of the cemetery.

My muscles trembled with the wavering walls, the pain in my dislocated shoulder screaming with my magical exertion. I tugged from Mayhem's grasp, breaking our magical hold, and everyone around us gasped.

"I had it." Adrian glared at me, his hands curling into fists. "I could have ended him with its power."

"There are six of us and two of you." I rested my hand on my hip, wishing I could cross my arms. "What are you going to do?"

He sniffed, lifting his chin like a spoiled, stubborn child. "Where did your griffin take it?"

"It's not our griffin, and I have no idea." But I hoped to Hecate our demons did because, otherwise, we were screwed.

Adrian moved his chin from side to side like a cow chewing cud. "Let's go, Gray. You've got scrying to do."

She swallowed hard. "What about Hector?"

"Leave him for the vultures," he said, locking his gaze with mine for a moment before he turned and walked away.

"Was he trying to say we're the vultures?" I asked.

"Half of what he says doesn't make sense," Gray whispered, hesitating to follow her leader. "Will you...?"

She moved toward me, lowering her voice even more. "I know you don't owe us anything, but will you cremate him? The thought of him being eaten is..." She visibly shuddered.

I wanted to tell her to go eff herself because she was right. We didn't owe them a damn thing. But if that were one of my friends laying dead on the ground and I didn't have the power to do it myself, I'd probably ask the same thing.

Nobody deserved to get eaten.

"We'll take care of him," I said.

"On one condition," Mayhem added. "You must distract Adrian. Do whatever you can to stall him so that we may reach the amulet first."

"I..." Fear rounded her eyes, and her lower lip trembled.

"Just go." I rolled my eyes. "Bow to your master, kiss his ring or suck his toes, or whatever the hell it is you do. We don't need your help."

She gave me a blubbery nod and scurried away, leaving us to deal with the bodies of an overgrown bug and the unfortunate witch who'd gotten in his way.

CHAPTER 14
EMBER

"Holy Hecate. What day is it?" I leaned on the steering wheel, squinting at the sea of brake lights ahead of us.

"It's the twenty-ninth. Halloween is the day after tomorrow," Ash said, her voice grim. I had never felt such ominous doom coming from my little sister, but she had every reason to embody it.

Halloween was the biggest tourist day of the year in Salem. The day humans packed themselves into our quiet little town like a can of biscuits waiting to burst. The day the normally thinnest part of the veil became its absolute thinnest, and they had no clue it was all about to fall apart.

I'd seen it. When I'd held Mayhem's hand and we'd shared our magic, the veil itself had become visible to me. I'd felt it too. Even in Worcester, seventy miles from Salem, the entire fabric of reality was about to unravel around us.

And an effing griffin had taken the one thing that could've saved us all.

"How is your shoulder?" Mayhem asked from the passenger seat.

"It's fine." I waved off his concern. Yes, it had hurt like a beast while it was dislocated, but once Ash popped it back into place and applied her healing salve, I couldn't even tell I'd been injured.

It had taken a good half hour to cremate the fae, but Hector had turned into ashes in seconds. I felt bad for using my boot to spread his remains in a cemetery so far from home, but I sure as shit wasn't packing him into a box and returning him to Adrian the asshat.

"Come on, people." I laid on the horn, though I knew it would do no good. Traffic inched forward, and my fatigue inched further and further up my spine, threatening to pull me under. If we could just make it two more blocks, I could take a side street and get us home.

In the meantime, we might as well make use of our time. "Tell me what you know about griffins."

"Who are you asking?" Shade said from the way back seat.

"Anyone who knows anything." I tightened my grip on the wheel. "Why would it take the amulet?"

"I'm searching the witchy web," Ash said. "It's

hard to distinguish between what's real, what's popular fiction, and what every random Dungeon Master in the D and D world has made up about them."

"The griffin took the amulet for one simple reason," Mayhem said. "They like shiny things."

I barked out a laugh. "Wait. Are you serious?"

"She was probably drawn to its power as well," Chaos said. "And to ours."

Mayhem nodded. "Three beings of royal descent in one place. A High Priestess and Priest from rival covens. Air and fire magic. I'm surprised the griffin and the fae were the only ones who got through."

"I thought the more power a being has, the harder it is to cross over," Miles said.

I leaned my forehead on the steering wheel and closed my eyes. "Hecate's hold is slipping. Remember Cinder's letter? They're doing what they can to keep it intact, but 'even the goddess can't hold it forever.'"

A horn blared behind me, the offending noise like a dagger to my eardrums. I jerked my head up as a blue SUV jutted onto the shoulder and passed me, filling in the single car length I'd let grow between our van and the sedan in front of us.

"Asshole." I straightened, leaning my neck from side to side, stretching the tension in my muscles. Mayhem reached across the console and dug his thumb into the sorest spot as if he could feel exactly what hurt.

He massaged from the base of my skull, down to my shoulder, and back up again before letting go and winking. "I'll get the other side for you when we're home."

I grinned. "You better. Because now I'm lopsided." How odd was it that I could still enjoy the flutter in my belly his flirting caused? If I were a good High Priest-ess, my thoughts would have been laser-focused on saving my coven. Instead, giddiness bubbled in my gut from simply being near him.

"I found an article on Witchipedia," Ash said. "It has links to sources, so maybe it's true."

"What does it say?" I inched the car forward, nearly kissing the SUV's backside as I turned on my brights.

Mayhem laughed. "You are much more patient than I am. He'd be missing a bumper by now if I were driving."

"Can we not cause a fender bender tonight?" Ash glared at me through the rearview mirror. "We have enough on our plates."

I dimmed my lights. "What does the article say?"

"Griffins reside in the Underworld and rarely cross the veil." Ash slid her finger up her screen, scrolling the page. "Females line their nests with gems and other shiny objects so they can find them from the sky."

"Does the Underworld have a sky?" I asked.

Mayhem chuckled. "You know our realm isn't actually *under* yours, right? We don't live in a cave in the ground. It's another dimension, parallel to yours."

I gave him the side eye. "Of course I know that."

"Then why did you ask?" He arched a teasing brow.

My belly fluttered again. "Because I'm tired and lopsided. So the griffin is making a nest somewhere in this realm. What else?"

"They nest in the mountains." Ash continued to scroll. "When her eggs hatch, she'll nurse her young until their wings are strong enough for them to fly away."

"Nurse?" Shade sounded perplexed. "A mammal who lays eggs. What other anomalies do you have in the Underworld?"

"It's not that unusual," I said. "Platypi are mammals who lay eggs."

"Platypuses is the right way to make it plural," Ash said.

"Thank you, grammar police." I blew out a hard breath. "You know what? Screw this."

I jerked the wheel to the right and plowed up the shoulder to turn down a side street. The main road was normally the fastest route home, but there was nothing normal about...well...about this entire year. I took the back roads, going the long way around

Salem so we could enter the town from behind the mess.

"So, we have a momma griffin about to lay eggs, the key to our salvation lays in her nest, and we have no idea where she decided to build it. We can scry for it, but how the hell will we get to it on the top of a mountain? And how will we get her and her eggs back to Hell?"

"Griffins are generally docile creatures. They won't attack unless you agitate them...like trolls." Chaos gave me a look, and yeah, okay, I deserved it.

I had agitated a troll, and we'd had to kill the poor beastie because of me. But I was getting better at not causing trouble. Someone should've acknowledged my progress, right? Baby steps were still steps, and I was a changed woman. I was in the process of becoming one, anyway.

"If she's already laid her eggs, us just getting near her nest will upset her." Ash swiped away the article and laid her phone in her lap. "Moms are vicious protectors of their babies."

I turned left and made my way up the alley, a sense of relief washing over me as I pulled into the driveway behind our house. I allowed myself to feel peace for a moment before opening the door and sliding out of the van.

"Tonight, we sleep." I opened the hidey hole and

pulled out my sword. "Tomorrow morning, we scry. After that...I guess we're climbing a mountain."

"You have no idea the mountains we will have to climb." Mayhem slid his arm around my waist and took the duffel bag from my hand.

"That's why we're going to scry." I grabbed another bag of equipment and headed for the door.

"There are things you need to know." He lowered his voice to a whisper and walked beside me. "We'll talk inside."

Well, that didn't sound ominous at all. Honestly though, I was too tired to talk. At the moment, my one priority was snuggling with my demon and falling asleep in his arms. Something I wanted to do every night for the rest of my life. My heart wrenched at the thought.

This could be the last night I ever spent with Mayhem. *Ever.* Halloween was in two days. Once the sun came up, we'd have until midnight to get the amulet, summon Discord, bring back my family, and mend the veil.

Then...he'd be gone forever.

If we failed? The curse would come to fruition, and Ash would kill me...if the veil didn't unravel and kill us all first. Either way, fate would tear us apart. *Fickle, fickle bitch.*

A sob rolled up from deep within my soul, but I caught it in my throat. I tried to swallow it, but the damn thing was the size of a baseball. Tears gathered on my lower lids as I led the way upstairs. I could not let my team see me like this.

"Set your alarms," I said as I dropped the bag onto the counter and tugged Mayhem toward the hall. I caught a glimpse of Ash before I turned into my bedroom, and the expression on her face nearly made me lose it.

She realized what was about to happen too.

I dragged my demon into my room and locked the door before hanging my sword above the bed. A tear slid down my cheek, and I wiped it away, trying to compose myself before I turned to face him.

He rested his hands on my shoulders. "We will figure out a way."

"Will we?" The sob hanging out in my throat finally surfaced, racking my entire body as it flowed past my lips.

He squeezed my left shoulder, massaging it for a second before sliding his arms around me, pulling my back against his front. "Bringing your sister back will be difficult at best, but it can be done."

I laugh/sobbed as another tear rolled down my cheek, and I twisted in his arms to face him. "That's not what I'm thinking about right now."

His lips parted, sadness softening his eyes. "We will figure out a way for us as well."

"Don't." I rested my palms on his chest, pushing

him away. "I don't need you to lie to me. We both know how this has to end. I just wish..."

He pulled me to his chest, wrapping his arms around me firmly. "I will do whatever it takes."

I leaned into him, laying my head on his shoulder and letting him hold me. "I just wish I'd accepted all this sooner. Deep down, I think I knew from the moment we summoned you. I wasted so much time."

"Nothing has been wasted." He tucked my hair behind my ear and kissed the side of my head. "We are together here, now, in this moment. We should cherish it."

He was right. I'd been so busy thinking about next steps, planning, leading... I'd become High Priestess and lost myself. Before everything happened, I lived in the moment. I appreciated little things, experiences. I needed to bring that part of me back. It was the only way I'd survive the aftermath.

I pulled away to look at him, and another tear slid down my cheek. "I love you, Mayhem."

He wiped it with his thumb and smiled softly. "And I love you."

Rising onto my toes, I pressed my lips to his. He held me tighter, neither of us moving, both of us frozen in a combined state of despair, determination, and downright anger. His lips parted, and he kissed me harder, bringing his hand to the back of my head before touching his forehead to mine and closing his eyes.

"We will…" he began.

"Please don't." My throat thickened. "If I keep thinking, it will paralyze me. Just…"

I stepped out of his embrace and traced my finger over his sigil. "I know I'll have to remove this before you go home. Promise you'll never forget about me."

My throat, my heart, my stomach, my soul…every fiber of my being twisted and turned, my nerves and emotions so raw, I could have melted into a puddle on the floor without noticing.

Mayhem's Adam's apple bobbed, his lips parting and closing like he wanted to keep assuring me that we'd be together forever and always. But he knew better too. "For the rest of my existence, not a single moment will ever pass when I don't think about you."

He stepped toward me and cupped my face in his hand, kissing me slowly, purposely, drinking me in like…no, not like…*because* this could be the last chance he would get.

I slipped my hands beneath his shirt, my fingertips memorizing the cuts and dips of his muscles, the silkiness of the trail of hair leading downward from his navel. Firm sinew contrasting with soft skin. The creature from Hell simmering beneath the surface of the most amazing man I had ever met.

"Why?" My voice trembled. "Goddess, why did it have to happen this way?"

"Hecate had nothing to do with this. Fate wove our story long before she was born." He grabbed the back of his shirt and tugged it over his head, dropping it on the floor.

Stop thinking, Ember. Enjoy this moment and forget it's the last. I kicked off my boots and continued memorizing his body with my hands and my eyes.

And my tongue.

I kissed his chest and ran my fingers down his arms to lace with his. His nipples hardened beneath my tongue, and as my teeth grazed one, he sucked in a breath. Releasing his hands, I took off my shirt and bra, tossing them next to his discarded shirt.

His pupils dilated, and he licked his lips, slowly unbuttoning his pants and shoving them to the floor. We continued undressing, our gazes never straying from each other's, until every article of clothing we'd worn lay in a heap next to my bed.

We stood there for a moment, looking at each other, once again frozen in the moment. He caressed every inch of my body with his gaze, and I inhaled deeply, reveling in his low vibration as it washed over me.

Based on past experience, this was the part where his pupils should constrict. He should prowl toward me, he, the predator, I, his prey. Instead, he gently trailed his fingers up my arms to my shoulders.

He stepped closer, a look of adoration in his eyes that nearly made me turn into that puddle after all. I sat on the mattress, moving to the center as he crawled on top of me and covered my body with his. The warmth of his skin and his spiced, fiery scent made my head spin in a good way, the passion-drunk look in his eyes telling me he enjoyed the same things from me.

Never in my life had I needed anyone the way I needed him now. I wanted all of him. I wanted to give him my all in return, so I opened to him, allowing my magic to rise to the surface and flow from me to him. Not just through our joined hands like normal. No, this time I let my magic seep from every inch of skin touching his.

A soft growl rumbled in his chest, and one corner of his mouth lifted into a lopsided, satisfied grin before he kissed me, slipping his tongue into my mouth to tangle with mine.

He glided a hand downward, between us, and teased my folds. He slid one finger inside me, then a second, and I gasped, the sensation stronger than I had ever felt before.

"Your sense of touch is heightened while you share your magic with me." He pulled them out to circle my clit before sliding them back inside.

"Ya think?" I laughed, not because it was funny, but because this was yet another experience I wished I'd had before tonight.

"I know." He pulled his fingers out and pressed his tip against me. "I can see it in your eyes." With a deep inhale, he opened himself to me, allowing his energy to wash over me, to meld with mine.

It felt like I was coming to life. Like my first twenty-seven years on Earth were just a dress rehearsal, and now, this demon was showing me how to live. My skin turned to gooseflesh as our breaths found the same rhythm and our hearts beat in unison.

He filled me with one swift thrust, and we became one. One heart, one body, one soul. Fate had bound us together, and I knew in that moment I would never love another man. I couldn't if I tried.

He made love to me slowly, his gaze never straying from mine, the adoration in his eyes palpable as we shared our bodies and our magic. His every touch electrified me, the delicious friction as he moved inside me like nothing I had ever felt before.

My core tightened, the orgasm exploding through my body without warning, setting my nerves ablaze. I gasped at the sensation, and he moaned his approval, but his rhythm didn't cease.

He kept going, kissing one side of my neck, and then the other, tangling his fingers in my hair as he pumped his hips faster. Another wave of ecstasy crashed through me, tearing apart my being and weaving it back together, stronger than it was before.

The third time I came, he did too. He groaned, his face contorting with pleasure as he slammed into me three times before burying himself so deeply, we could have actually become one being.

He collapsed on top of me, nuzzling into my neck, our hearts still beating in unison, our breaths slowing as we came down from the climax together.

"This time was different." He drew his magic inward and rose onto his elbows. "You tamed the demon in me."

I smiled and brushed a strand of hair from his forehead. "I would never try to tame you. Whether you're in demon or human form doesn't matter. They're both you, and I love them both equally."

Anguish flashed in his eyes before he rolled to his back and pulled me to his side. "I can't imagine existing without you."

"Then don't imagine it. Hold me like the night will last forever." I rested my head on his chest and draped my leg across his hips. "Feel everything now so you'll never forget."

He kissed the top of my head. "A million years could pass, and this moment would be as fresh in my thoughts as it is now."

"Good." I snuggled closer and tried not to fall asleep. I wanted to cherish the moment, to bask in it for as long as possible, but Morpheus had other plans for me.

I couldn't say how long the god of sleep gave me before he dragged me under, but the morning sunlight slicing across my eyes couldn't be ignored. Never had I ever been so reluctant to wake up and start my day, but I had to.

I blinked open my eyes and found my demon lying on his side, watching me sleep. "Good morning," he said. I didn't miss the sadness in his voice.

"I guess it's time to bring Cinder home." I ran a hand down my face and lightly slapped my cheeks, trying to wake myself up. "After we complete all the other tasks on the list."

His brow furrowed. "Once we obtain the rest of the amulet, summoning Discord should be simple."

"Thank the goddess for that." I pushed to sitting.

"But there is something you need to know about your sister." He sat up, his gaze searching mine. There was something in his eyes. Something...off.

"What do I need to know?"

"She's..." He blew out a hard breath. "Cinder is dead."

I laughed.

He didn't.

"What?" I pressed the sheets to my chest and scooted toward the edge of the bed. "Are you serious?"

"I'm afraid so."

CHAPTER 15
MAYHEM

"How could she be dead?" Ember's brows drew together, her eyes rounding. "She's a Holland. She's powerful enough to survive the transition across the veil. It wouldn't shred her. It couldn't. She sent us a letter. She…"

"No one truly survives the transition to Hell." I reached for her hand, but she pulled away.

"And you're just now telling me this?" Her voice held a shrill edge. "The whole plan all along was to summon both of them. To bring Discord *and* Cinder back to this realm and then bring back our parents. Why…?"

"To be fair, I've tried to have this discussion with you on several occasions. I—"

She shot me a fiery glare that cut the words off in

my throat. Perhaps now wasn't the time for my defense.

"So, she's dead. Stuck in Hell for all eternity?" She rose and gathered our discarded clothes, dropping them into a hamper.

Gods, she was beautiful. Sunlight filtering through the blinds illuminated her fair skin, giving her an ethereal glow. Three faint scars marred her stomach, claw marks, no doubt, but they didn't take away from her beauty. They showed her strength.

"Hello? My eyes are up here." She snapped her fingers, drawing me from the trance her exquisiteness had put me into. "Can we bring her back?"

"It's possible." I rose and straightened the bedsheets.

"Care to elaborate?" She crossed her arms.

"It's true a witch of her caliber can retain her corporeal form when she passes through to Hell. I have no doubt your sister's body remained intact. Your mother's too. I don't know your father's lineage, so his survival is questionable."

A pained look flashed across her face. "You really need to work on your delivery."

"I'm sorry. I don't know how else to put it." I strode to the dresser and took out a clean set of clothing. "There is hope."

"What will it take to bring them all back?" She

gathered a stack of clothes and strode into the bathroom.

I followed, pausing in the doorway to dress. "Unless you wish to employ a necromancer—and break every law your higher power has created for your kind—their safe passage to this realm will require the most demanding act of magic you have ever cast."

"I can deal with that." She shoved her toothbrush into her mouth and scrubbed.

"It will also require Lucifer's blessing."

She spat into the sink and rinsed her mouth. "Lucky for us, we have a direct line to the King of Hell. You can call him up and ask, right? Easy-peasy."

"If only it were." I joined her in the bathroom to brush my teeth as she finished dressing. "We've been absent from our posts for four centuries because of our involvement with a witch. He is angry with us at best. Convincing him to assist us with yet another witch encounter will not be easy."

She laughed dryly. "Witch encounter? You make us sound like aliens."

I shrugged. "To our realm, you are." I brushed my teeth and returned the toothbrush to the stand.

Ember padded to the bedroom and put on her boots. "And if we went the necromancy route, could we bring them back without his blessing?"

"Yes, but you would face the consequences of your Higher Power if you were caught. You would suffer in this life and then face Lucifer's wrath when your time here is through."

"We'll figure it out. I'll do whatever it takes to save my family." She strode toward the door and stopped, turning to me and resting a hand on her hip. "Don't tell them she's dead. It's possible to bring her back, so she's still alive to us. Got it?"

"I do."

"And don't mention necromancy or requiring Lucifer's blessing. Don't mention anything because we can't accomplish any of it without the amulet. We have to focus on one thing at a time."

"Understood. And I will work on my delivery for future bad news."

She shook her head. "We don't have time for more bad news. Let's go scry for the amulet."

I followed her to the kitchen, where she filled a copper bowl with water before setting it in the center of the table. She gathered candles and herbs and readied the space for scrying while we waited for the others to join us.

Chaos and Ash were the first to arrive, and Ash went straight to the coffee machine, starting the brew before nodding at Ember's setup. "I need some caffeine in me before we do this."

We remained silent, listening to the machine rumble as the water dripped into the carafe.

"Oh, good. Coffee," Miles said as he and Shade entered the room. "I was thinking..."

"Careful..." Ember took six mugs from the cabinet. "Too much of that can get you into trouble."

He chuckled. "Right?"

Shade sat at the table. "Doesn't it seem odd that the griffin showed up exactly when it did? It was too random to actually be random."

"You think someone summoned it?" Ember poured the coffee into mugs and handed one to me.

"It's just a thought." Miles carried two mugs to the table and sat next to Shade. "Chrys summoned the basilisk to slow us down. Maybe Adrian or the fae summoned the griffin."

"I'm still impressed that you fought such a beast." I poured sugar into my coffee and stirred it with a small spoon before taking my seat at the table. "Taking on the griffin will be easy-peasy." I winked at Ember as I used her expression.

She fought a grin and sat next to me. "Assuming the griffin still has the amulet. If Ignacus or Adrian summoned it, they could've already taken it and sent the griffin on her way."

"Well, then..." Ash sat down and gulped her drink before holding out her hands. "Let's find out."

Ember slipped her palm into mine, but Shade hesitated, his gaze flicking from my face to my hand.

"What's wrong?" Miles asked, taking Shade's and Chaos's hands.

"My energy overwhelmed him in the vault," I said.

"It didn't overwhelm me." He laid a tight fist on the table. "I'm just not used to it like she is."

"Let's trade places." Ember tapped me on the shoulder. "I'll filter it for you."

"Perhaps Chaos and I should sit this one out." I rose and pushed my chair beneath the table.

"We can't do it without you." Ember twisted in her seat and grabbed my hand, the desperate look on her face giving me pause, making me want to sit down again and hold her hand. To hold on to her for eternity.

But the only way I knew to make that happen would be whisking her away to the Underworld. I took a breath, imagining the centuries we could spend together. Then I thought of what our passage through...that of a demon prince and an elemental witch...would do to the veil. What it would do to her world and everyone in it.

"Yes, you can." I tugged from her grasp. "You've been scrying without us for years. You don't need our help."

Hurt flashed in her eyes, and I quickly continued,

softening my delivery. "I say this for your team's sake. You were built to handle every part of me, my magic included. Think of what it felt like when you channeled Chaos's power and double it...quadruple it. That's what it feels like for them."

She stared at me, not saying a word.

I rested a hand on her shoulder. "Your team needs you to do this without us."

"You've gotten used to the extra power boost," Shade said, "but once they're gone, you'll have to live without it. Might as well get used to it."

Ember's neck stiffened, her shoulders drawing inward slightly. She tried to mask her reaction to Shade's words knifing her heart, but she could not hide her feelings from me. Anger at his callousness simmered in my chest. This was what Ember meant about delivery. Shade had stated a fact about which there was no dispute, but his choice of words and tone of voice had caused my witch unnecessary anguish.

I was tempted to plant my fist on his jaw, but I refrained. Acting on my instincts in such a way would only make our quest harder.

"Shall we, brother?" I motioned toward the door before I lost my ability to abstain.

Chaos stood and rested his hands on Ash's shoulders, bending to kiss her cheek before following me into the kitchen. "We'll be downstairs."

We left the witches to their scrying and descended

the steps, stopping in the library. He picked up a stack of tomes and carried them to a bookcase, but he didn't put them on the shelf. Instead, he set them on the floor and retrieved the feather duster lying haphazardly in the middle of an aisle.

"How did you and Ember stop us all from fighting in the cemetery? Even I felt the urge to make peace when you channeled her magic." He swiped the feathers across the shelf, making dust billow in the air. Frowning, he dropped the duster and opened a cabinet containing cleaning supplies.

"We mimicked you." I shrugged and paced in front of the desk. "She held my hand and focused her magic into my mark. It mixed with mine, and I sent it outward. Same as you and Ash."

My brother sprayed a fine mist onto the shelf and used disposable towels to wipe away the dust. "We can only affect one person at a time. What you did was nothing short of impressive. Good work."

I opened my mouth, ready to retaliate with a quip, but I closed it again, turning on my heel and pacing away from him. I couldn't remember a time when he'd paid me a compliment. I had no idea how to respond.

"We must find a way to return to this realm after we mend the veil," I said. "I cannot exist without Ember. She is as essential as the air I breathe."

Chaos lined the books on the shelf. "I've been considering our options for weeks." He sprayed another shelf with cleaning fluid and wiped the dust. "The outcome will be grim at best."

"There must be something we can do." I continued pacing, clasping my hands behind my back. "The witches belong to us. With us. Fate would not send the missing pieces to our souls only to rip them away. Perhaps Lucifer..."

Chaos laughed dryly. "We've been away from our posts for too long. We'll be lucky to receive his blessing to bring Cinder back."

My heart sank. "I know."

Silence descended upon us, only the sounds of my brother's cleaning and my footsteps filling the room as the gravity of our predicament pressed harder on our shoulders.

If the fate of our eternal happiness rested on Lucifer's whims, we were...as Ember so eloquently put it...royally screwed.

"I believe he'll allow Cinder to return for the simple fact that he wants the veil to remain intact," Chaos finally said. "I highly doubt he'll allow their parents safe passage. They made a deal with a demon and must face the consequences."

My stomach soured. "Cinder did as well. Ash and Ember too."

Chaos stopped cleaning. I stopped pacing. We stood there, our gazes locked, each of us waiting for the other to spout a brilliant solution. My heart sank deeper and deeper, taking a swim in my stomach until the vise yanked it back to my chest, clenching it until I was certain it would burst.

I peered at the floor, willing an idea...or even an inkling of one...to form in my mind. Aside from dropping to our knees and begging Lucifer for mercy, I had nothing.

"I love her." I forced the words over the lump in my throat.

"I know." He tossed the towels into a trash bin and sank into the desk chair. "I love Ash too, but the only solution I can think of is taking them to Hell with us."

"Ember would never agree to that."

"Neither would Ash. I already asked her." He opened the drawer and pulled out the small, rolled parchment Cinder had sent across the veil. He used two fingers to unroll it, but he let it go, allowing it to return to its previous state.

"I am sorry for the Cerberus incident," he said, "and for joining Discord in mocking you. You've shown immeasurable restraint in this realm. Your strength is formidable, and I'm proud to call you my brother."

Again with the compliments. My gut reaction was to throw an insult his way, but I had noticed a change in him as well. Being in this realm had changed us both.

No, the realm had nothing to do with it. "Ember makes me a better man."

"As Ash does me." He unrolled the parchment again and scanned the words. "Hopefully Discord has a plan. He's been in touch with Hecate at the very least."

I stood behind him and read the letter over his shoulder, scanning the last three sentences repeatedly:

There's an amulet somewhere on your side. You have to find it and summon Discord so he can return it to its rightful owner. I can't come home without it.

"He's already done it." I leaned forward and tapped the final lines. "The rightful owner is Lucifer. Discord has bargained for Cinder's safe passage home, and the amulet is the price he'll pay."

"Maybe." Chaos returned the scroll to the drawer. "But the amulet belongs to Hecate as much as it does Lucifer. The goddess has been holding the veil together. Perhaps Cinder bargained with her, promising the amulet in return for her assistance while Ash and Ember complete their quests in this realm."

My heart sank yet again. That idea made more sense. Hecate was livid when Lucifer lost the amulet to Discord, and she had held the grudge for centuries.

"Speculating is pointless." I walked the width of

the room before turning around and striding back. "At this point, it doesn't matter to whom Discord plans to give the amulet. We don't have all of it, so we should focus on retrieving the final piece."

"Hey, guys," Ember said, descending halfway down the stairs. "We found it. Come on up."

CHAPTER 16
EMBER

"The griffin has it, but she's on the move." I paced in front of the television while the others took seats in the living room, just like old times. Well, all but Mayhem.

"How do you know she's on the move?" He stood between the kitchen and living room, shifting his weight from foot to foot, more restless than I'd ever seen him.

"We felt the amulet in motion when we scried," I said. "When we pulled back, we saw her flying. She hasn't laid her eggs yet, so we assume she's looking for a place to nest."

"Or for a way home," Ash said.

I nodded. "She seems agitated. She knows she needs to nest, but something is stopping her."

"How do you know she hasn't laid her eggs?"

Mayhem took a few steps toward me before dropping into his usual chair. "Perhaps she's searching for food."

"Her belly is distended, and her mannerisms say she's about to give birth." I stopped pacing and rested my hands on my hips. "So, the question is, how do we call to her and convince her Salem is the place she needs to be?"

"The veil is thinnest here, even with Hecate's magic holding it together," Ash said. "If she's looking for an easy path to the Underworld, this is where she'll find it."

"But if she's going to nest in this realm," Miles said, "Salem isn't the place. We have over a million tourists coming and going this time of year. Every hotel within twenty miles is completely booked. It's loud."

"You're right. It's way too noisy for nesting here." I sank onto the arm of Mayhem's chair and tapped a finger to my lips as an idea formed in my mind. It was a terrible, horrible, no-good idea, but it was the only one I had.

"The griffin is from the Underworld. I know she's not a demon, but can you call to her? Will she be attracted to your power?"

"All creatures from the Underworld are attracted to our power, especially in this realm," Mayhem said. "But she won't blindly obey us like a demon would.

She will need an incentive to come here, even if we connect with her."

"And the noise of the city will scare her away," Chaos said. "Griffins are docile, solitary creatures. She'll choose quiet over whatever we have to offer."

"Maybe not." I stood and resumed pacing. "We'll head to the outskirts of Salem, past the residential area and into the woods where tourists rarely go."

"Where we fought the shedim," Ash said. "It's quiet there, but the guys said we need some incentive to convince her to come. What are you thinking? A mound of birdseed?"

"Griffins are carnivorous," Mayhem said. "A mound of raw meat would entice her more than seeds, but not enough to draw her here. You have something else in mind, don't you?"

He flashed a conspiratorial grin, making my stomach flutter. "You want to open a rift, an invitation for her to go home."

I smiled in return. "That's exactly what I want to do."

"You're both crazy." Ash shot to her feet. "Are you sure I'm the one who's cursed? Because that maniacal grin you're sharing...? You look like you both need to be hit with a binding spell and a straitjacket."

"Opening rifts is what started all this trouble," Miles said. "I don't think creating another one is going to solve our problems, especially this close to Halloween."

"That's the worst idea I've ever heard," Shade said.

"It's brilliant," Mayhem said. "She'll head straight for the rift. We'll intercept the amulet, usher her through, and seal it behind her."

"It sounds easy enough," Chaos said.

Ash parked her hands on her hips, looking from me to the demons as if we'd grown eyeballs where our ears should be. "Name one thing about this entire ordeal that has happened easily."

I inhaled, ready to spout a string of answers, but not a single one came to mind. Nobody said a word as we looked at each other. Shade's brow furrowed in concentration, and Miles drew his shoulders upward, lifting his hands and looking just like the *I don't know* emoji on my phone.

"Exactly. But..." Ash dropped onto the couch next to Chaos. "I don't have a better idea. Anyone else?"

"No." Miles sank further into his seat, and Shade shook his head.

"Then we're in agreement. Let's—" My phone buzzed, so I dug it out of my pocket. Patrice's name lit up the screen as I swiped it open.

"Hey, you're on speaker." I set the device on the coffee table. "How are things?"

She missed a beat before she replied. "Tomorrow is Halloween."

"We're aware," I said. "How's your team doing? Everyone still accounted for?"

"So far, but activity is picking up. We took out a horde of vampire ghouls last night."

I tapped my foot on the floor. "That's standard stuff. Has anything bigger gotten through? Any trouble with the fae?"

"Not recently, but tomorrow is Halloween," she said again.

I rubbed my forehead, wishing people would stop stating the obvious and offer solutions instead.

Rustling sounded through the phone, followed by a cabinet opening and closing. "I ran out of wolfsbane and stopped by your house yesterday to borrow some, but I couldn't get in. Why the super strong wards? Did you find all the amulet pieces?"

"No, but we'll have them by the end of the day. Stay vigilant. Things will get worse before we make it all better."

She hesitated. "So the demons are…"

"Sitting right here," Ash said.

"Oh, okay… Who has the missing piece?" Patrice asked.

"A griffin. Long story." I grabbed the phone. "Did you have anything else to report?"

"No, that's it."

"Keep us posted. We'll do the same." I hit End and returned it to my pocket.

"Poor Patrice," Ash said. "She's a healer thrust into a fighting position."

"We've all had to step out of our comfort zones." I rose and headed toward the hall to get my sword. "Gather your things. We need to summon a griffin."

AFTER ASH RESTOCKED her spell kit and gave us speed and strength sigils, we loaded our weapons into the van and headed for the woods where we'd encountered our first demon. Of course, now I knew the shedim wasn't Ash's first demon. She'd already summoned Chaos and brought him along for the ride, but that didn't matter now. I might be dead if he hadn't taken up residence in her mind, so who was I to complain?

I parked along the side of the road, and we filed out, gathering our knives and swords and bundles of enchanted rope before creeping deeper into the trees. Clouds blanketed the sky, casting the forest in an eerie shade of washed-out gray, and dry leaves crunched beneath my boots as we made our way to the clearing.

No remnants of the teens' poorly cast circle remained. If I didn't know the story, I'd have no clue a mid-level demon had feasted on a wannabe witch's makeshift coven nearly a month ago.

To be fair, we'd had nothing to do with those kids summoning the shedim. They'd done that all on their own, but I doubt they would have accomplished it if we—my family—hadn't already thinned the veil and started this mess into motion.

I couldn't bring myself to count the number of bodies we'd left in our wake. The sheer amount of death and destruction, caused by the very people who were supposed to keep Salem safe, seemed infinite. I paused, letting my team walk ahead of me.

Mayhem stayed by my side. "What troubles you?"

I laughed dryly. "Take your pick."

He rested a hand on my hip. "This is something new. Tell me what you're thinking."

I shrugged one shoulder and shook my head. "I don't want to believe this is all happening because of us. My family. If our mom would have been honest with us from the start, if Cinder hadn't taken matters into her own hands... We caused this."

"No, Isabel caused this when she cursed your bloodline. The Holland witches are not to blame."

"Do you know why she cursed our bloodline? Did she ever tell you?"

He lowered his gaze. "I never asked."

Something between a sob and a laugh rolled up from my chest. "She cursed us because my great-great-times-however-many-greats grandma stole her man and founded the coven she was planning to build."

I waited for him to respond, but he remained silent.

"So, yeah... The Holland witches are to blame." I stepped toward the others, but he grasped my hand.

"I'm sure your ancestor had no way of knowing the ramifications, and anyway..." He cupped my chin in his hand, bringing my gaze to his. "When fate brings two people together, there is no use fighting it."

"Don't you dare give me the 'everything happens for a reason' spiel."

"Some things do. Some don't. We shouldn't focus on what might have been while ignoring what is. That kind of thinking paralyzes people. Believe me, I know." He dropped his hand to his side.

"Are you ready, brother?" Chaos called from the clearing.

Mayhem looked at me, silently arching a brow. He was right. Guilt was a paralyzing, useless emotion, and we didn't have time for my pity party. He offered his hand, and I took it, allowing him to lead me into the clearing to join our team.

I left my sword sheathed and tugged the rope I carried from my shoulder, adjusting the lasso end until it was balanced properly for throwing. "You're sure she won't try to eat us?"

"Not entirely." Mayhem moved next to Chaos.

I lowered the rope. "Not the answer I was expecting. You said they were docile."

"I said they were docile unless provoked," Chaos answered. "So don't provoke her."

"Because lassoing and hog-tying aren't provocational at all." I clenched my teeth, closing my eyes and reminding myself we were on the same team. "I'll try my best. At least they're not venomous."

I tilted my head and batted my lashes, giving my sister's demon the best demure face I could pull off. "Or are they?"

Mayhem chuckled. "They are not venomous, though their claws are razor-sharp and massive."

"Note to self: Steer clear of the murder mittens. Got it." I readjusted the rope. "She wasn't far from here when we scried. Do your thing, and we'll catch her."

"Hold on! I'm here," Patrice shouted as she scurried through the trees, her ginormous medical bag bouncing against her hip as she ran. "Sorry it took so long. I used the main road like a dummy."

She stopped in her tracks when she reached the edge of the clearing and smoothed her hair back into her ponytail. Her gaze cut between the demons a few times before she focused on Ash. "I've got sutures, salves, and everything in-between."

"Umm...?" I gave Ash a quizzical look.

"She texted and wanted to help." Ash adjusted her rope. "We're about to trap a magical combination of two apex predators, so I figured there might be injuries for her to heal."

"That's fair." I nodded.

"Plus Inga and Luis are driving me bonkers. You'd

think they were married with how much they argue." She let out a nervous laugh and took a tiny step away from the demons.

"Also fair," I said. "Mayhem and Chaos are about to work their demon magic to create a mental connection with the griffin. Once they do, they'll open a rift and invite her to go home. Before she passes through, we'll trap her and get the amulet. Then we'll let her go and seal the rift."

"Sounds better than getting covered in ghoul goo." She lifted the shoulder strap over her head and carried her bag to a nearby tree. "Why rope and not a binding spell?"

"Of the animals in the Underworld, griffins are near the top of the chain," Mayhem said. "A bind strong enough to hold a mother ready to lay eggs would deplete your vim for hours. I'm afraid we have very little time remaining to complete our quest."

She returned the bottle she'd grabbed to her bag and pulled out a set of green crystals instead. "I'll be ready if you need me."

"Everyone else ready?" I asked.

My team nodded, and I gave the demons a thumbs up. They closed their eyes and breathed deeply. Miles kept his gaze glued to the sky, while Shade's bounced between the demons and the treetops. Ash stared at Chaos intently while Patrice dug through her bag, doing her best to ignore the palpable low vibration building in the air.

At least, the vibration was palpable to me. I watched Mayhem work, a sense of peace washing over me as he and his brother called to a beastie that could murder me with a single swipe of her mitten.

Crazy, I know, but the man had that effect on me.

I focused on the sigil glowing softly on my arm, and his vibration grew stronger around me, inside me. I could feel him reaching out into the ether, searching for the griffin's signature, and when he found her, it felt as if I had found her too.

Her vibration was unmistakable, not as low and strong as the demons, but definitely not of this world. Ash inhaled quickly, no doubt feeling the same connection herself.

Our demons raised their arms in unison, swiping their hands from left to right, tearing through the fabric of the universe and creating a rift...an opening to Hell itself.

I gasped and pressed a hand to my chest as if the gesture could keep the air in my lungs...could keep my boots rooted to the ground.

The glowing red edges of the rift drifted farther apart, creating a massive hole in reality, the earthly realm on one side, utter darkness on the other. I couldn't ignore the pull. It drew me toward it, my feet moving of their own volition, the need to cross through it, to go *home*, so strong, I couldn't have fought it if I tried.

My vision tunneled until all I could see was my soulmate standing in front of the sure path to our happily ever after. My strides quickened, breaking into a run as the overwhelming call from the other side refused to be ignored.

"Ember, no." Mayhem caught me around the waist. "The rift is for the griffin, no one else."

"Don't you feel it?" I clutched his arm. "I know you feel it."

He gripped my shoulders, turning so I faced only him, my back to the rift. "Of course I feel it. I've felt the pull with every rift I've encountered, but I fight it."

"Why?" I grasped his shoulders too. "We can be together there. Forever, Mayhem. Isn't that what you want?"

His eyes searched mine, the purple in his irises growing fluid, pulsing, drawing me even further into the frenzied madness. "Forever in the Underworld," he said. "Is that what *you* want, Ember?"

"I..."

CHAPTER 17
EMBER

Fear flushed through me, turning my veins to ice and battling with the pull of the Underworld. My nails dug into Mayhem's shoulders as I tried to wrench myself free from his grasp.

He held onto me tighter. "That is the griffin's fear, not yours."

"The hell it is." I turned, yanking my shoulder away, but he refused to loosen his grip. "Let me go."

"Ember, stop." He ducked down to catch my gaze. "Breathe for me, my love. Breathe and focus inward. What do *you* feel?"

Icy veins, nausea, full-on flight mode. "Sheer terror."

"Ignore my sigil and look deeper." He released one shoulder to press his palm to my chest. "What do you feel here?"

I swallowed the thickness from my throat and focused on the sensation of his hand against my heart. His irises returned to their normal amethyst hue, and my pulse slowed to a manageable speed. "I…"

"Have you ever been afraid of me?"

I gave my head a tiny shake. "No."

"Mayhem…" Chaos's voice sounded strained.

My demon raised a finger to his brother, his gaze never straying from mine. "Are you afraid of me now?"

"No, I could never. I want to be with you always. We can if…" I tried to move toward the rift, but he held me tightly.

"Release your hold on me. Close the connection before the Underworld drags you through."

"I don't want to. We need to go through."

"You must. This is too much for your body to bear." He covered the sigil on my arm with his hand. "I'm not going anywhere, and neither are you. Please, Ember, shut it off."

I sucked in a shaky breath and focused on our connection, trying to close it, but the moment it grabbed my focus, I wanted nothing more than to run through the rift, taking my demon with me.

"Please, Mayhem. We have to go."

"No." His grip on my arm tightened, his brow slamming down over his eyes. "Close the connection, Ember. I demand it."

"I can't."

"You can, and you will." His eyes softened. "You must if you want to survive."

I gasped as the sensation of a heavy door slamming rocked my system. A moment of clarity brought the world into focus before the door cracked and my desire to drag him to Hell returned.

"Do it, Ember." He pushed the door closed once more.

My stomach churned and pain sliced through my veins like razors as I tried. I imagined the glow of his mark fading, leaving behind only the black ink from which it was created. Panting with the exertion, I mentally erased the ink, leaving my arm unmarred.

With another deep breath, I closed the connection, finally freeing myself from the grips of...*whatever* that was. "I don't. I don't understand."

"I don't have time to explain. I must help Chaos keep the rift in check." He kissed my forehead and released my arm. "Don't try to connect with me again. Not while this rift is open."

"Okay." My voice was barely audible over my pulse whooshing in my ears. "How...?"

He locked the imaginary door between us, severing our connection from his end and nearly ripping the breath from my lungs. I gasped and turned a circle, my lungs burning, my soul aching as if it had been torn in two...shredded. The rest of my team stared at me with concerned expressions. Even Ash.

"Did you not feel that?" I pointed at the demons.

Ash pursed her lips, her gaze flicking to my arm before she met my eyes. "I felt something, but definitely not whatever you felt."

I huffed, my mouth hanging open as I stood there dumbfounded. What the actual eff had just happened? One minute, I was poised and ready to rodeo with a griffin. The next, I wanted to leave everything behind and jump into the rift.

"She is here." Mayhem's voice sounded normal. No straining since he shared the load with his brother, but I didn't dare turn around to look at him. My legs felt numb, my mind mushy, and my insides tangled and twisted.

I squinted into the sky, but without Mayhem's magic flowing through me, I couldn't see the griffin above us. "Where?"

"She will arrive from the east," my demon said. "You must capture her before she makes it through the rift."

"That's the plan." Ash unwound her rope, holding the lasso by the loop. Miles and Shade did the same while Patrice mixed a healing potion.

My mouth still hung open, so I snapped it shut and shielded my eyes against the sun. I caught a glimpse of my forearm in my peripheral vision and sucked in the biggest, sharpest breath I had ever inhaled.

Mayhem's sigil was gone.

I checked my other arm, in case I'd forgotten where my demon's mark lay—as if that could happen —but only the speed and strength sigils Ash had applied remained on my skin. I rubbed my unmarred skin and glanced at Mayhem. The rift was now invisible to me, the urge to plow through it and spend eternity in Hell gone.

My brow crumpled as I caught Mayhem's gaze. "What did you do?"

"Incoming!" Miles said, drawing me back to our current predicament.

The griffin seemed to glow in the late morning sun, her white feathers gleaming, fading into shiny brown fur. She screeched, sending the forest critters scampering, and I widened my stance, my muscles tightening, my thoughts narrowing, pinpointing on my task.

Because if I stopped to think about what just happened with Mayhem, I might crumble into dust.

The beastie circled above us, half-screeching, half-roaring her disapproval. Shade threw his rope, yanking it back to tighten the loop when it hit her paw, but she flapped her wings, ascending before he could get ahold of her.

A growl rumbled from her chest, and she did a little loop-de-loop above us before perching at the top of a tree. Its branches groaned beneath her weight, a few of the smaller ones snapping and falling to the ground.

"Here, kitty, kitty." I crept toward the tree. "Pspspsp."

"Her head is an eagle." Shade rolled his eyes. "I doubt cat noises…"

"Reow," the griffin replied, her eyes darting in their sockets.

"She's scared. Can you calm her down?" I glanced at the demons.

"We will not harm you," Mayhem said. "Give us the amulet, and you are free to return to the Under-world, where you can nest in peace."

She let out a nervous mewl and adjusted her perch.

"Where is the amulet, guys?" Patrice inched toward the tree, pointing at each paw before circling her finger to indicate the griffin's beak. "I don't see it."

"Neither do I." I strode toward the beastie, my stomach souring. "She must've dropped it somewhere."

The griffin let out an ear-splitting screech. Her claws extended from her murder mittens, her giant bean-toes curling around the branches, snapping them as if they were twigs. I stumbled back as she scrambled to grab another branch, but the tree couldn't support her weight anymore.

She tumbled, smacking her head against the ground

before sitting up, stunned. I tossed my lasso, using her temporary immobility to loop it around her neck. She scrambled to her feet, and Ash got a loop around one paw.

"Why are we trapping her if she doesn't have the amulet?" Miles asked.

"She has it," Mayhem said. "I can sense it nearby."

"As can I," Chaos said, "but you must act quickly. If this rift gets any larger, we won't be able to stop the horde gathering on the other side."

"Big demons?" I tightened my loop.

"Many big demons," Mayhem said.

"It's okay, sweet girl." I inched closer, wrapping the rope around my hand to take up the slack as I approached. "Do you have a pouch somewhere or did you drop the amulet?"

She let out a nervous chuffing sound as she eyed our demons and the rift, stomping her paws like a bull ready to charge. I held up my hands, widening my stance and feeling an awful lot like the raptor-tamer guy from *Jurassic World*. There I was, trying to calm a ginormous animal that shouldn't even be in this world, when she could take my head off with one snap of her massive beak.

"What do we do, guys?" I took another step forward, and she growled. "Okay, I won't get any closer. Can you talk to her?" I looked over my shoulder at the demons.

"She's an animal," Mayhem said. "She understands as much as a house cat would."

Patrice said something under her breath. I snapped my gaze to her as she tossed a pint of blue liquid on the griffin's side. "She must have it!" Her voice took on a shrill edge, her eyes widening and her nostrils flaring as she recited a binding spell I'd never heard. "Ties that bind and control. With this spell, I have full hold."

The griffin jerked her head toward Patrice, yanking Ash's rope from her grasp. I'd coiled mine around my hand, so I kept my grip. But as the beastie roared and snapped at Patrice, she hauled me with her, knocking my feet out from under me and dragging me across the ground.

So much for the new binding spell.

Patrice screamed and stumbled into a tree. The griffin huffed and stomped, and Shade pulled out the enchanted dagger, pointing it at the beastie's rump and releasing a blast of Miles's energy.

She screeched and snapped at Shade, swiping out a paw. Lucky for Shade, the tip of her claw barely nicked his arm. Sure, she opened a massive gash in his biceps, but if she'd been five inches closer, she'd have sliced him in two.

"What happened to not agitating her?" I dusted off my pants.

The griffin unfurled her wings.

"Oh, shit."

She flapped, taking to the sky and—since I'd so brilliantly coiled the rope around my hand—dragging me along with her. I grabbed it with my free hand as she ascended, and I hung from her neck like a human albatross, swinging in the breeze as she circled just above the trees.

At least I was right-side-up this time.

"Can you see the amulet?" Chaos shouted from below. "Perhaps it's matted in her fur."

I gazed up at the momma-to-be. Her white eagle feathers blended perfectly into sleek, brown fur. Not a mat to be seen. Her belly was even bigger than the day before, and her udders...or were they called nipples on a lion? Whatever the proper term, they looked painfully red and swollen.

Something in her tummy shifted, her eggs, I assumed, and she let out a deep, distraught bellow that nearly broke my heart. This poor creature needed to nest...now.

"I don't think she has it," I shouted as I climbed the rope. What I planned to do when I reached the top, I wasn't sure, but I was too high to let go and fall. My legs would snap on impact from this altitude.

"She does," Mayhem said. "Use your magic to sense it. She has it somewhere on her person."

Oof. Yet another skill I hadn't practiced in a while. Ash was the one who scoured the thrift stores and collected magical artifacts before the humans could get their hands on them.

The griffin bellowed again and swooped toward a tree. Branches slapped across my arms, cutting into my skin, and I buried my face in her feathers as she unsteadily perched in an oak. The blob in her stomach shifted again, moving closer to the exit, and she huffed out a mewling moan.

"Hey, sweet girl. I'm not going to hurt you." I tentatively rested a hand on her shoulder, running it over her silky fur. "I just need to see if you have the amulet. I don't think you do, but the demons down there insist."

I grabbed a handful of fur and hauled myself onto her back. She made an irritated chuffing sound, and I stroked her, running my hands from her feathers to her fur and focusing on sending soothing energy into her.

"My love is wide, my caring deep. I wish you calm so you may sleep." My mom used to say those words to me when I was a kid and was too wound up for bedtime. My palms warmed, my peaceful intent seeping into her as I recited the spell again.

I continued petting the griffin and glanced at the scene below. The demons no longer strained, which meant they had closed the rift they'd opened. Shade sat with his back against a tree trunk while Patrice stitched up his arm, and Ash and Miles worked together on a potion.

The griffin began to relax, the tension in her muscles easing as my calming energy soothed her.

Me, calm and soothing. Crazy, I know.

With the beastie subdued, I shifted my focus to sensing the amulet. I lay on the griffin's back, resting my cheek against her feathered neck and spreading my arms, creating as much contact as I could. Her low, underworldly vibration registered in my psyche, growing stronger and stronger until my entire body hummed.

Wait. I lifted my head and smiled. That wasn't her magical vibration I felt. She was purring.

"That's a good girl." I laid my head on her neck and tried again. "Confess, expose my magic sleuth. I call on you to reveal your truth."

I didn't think the spell would actually work. Not without a potion to amplify my intent. But the moment the last word crossed my lips, I felt it. The griffin's magic was unmistakable, low and gray. She hadn't come to this realm with ill intent.

I felt Patrice's new binding spell too, though it was nothing like the one we normally used. This bind seemed to be more about controlling the receiver. Forcing compliance. It was an interesting choice for a healer witch, but we were all acting outside our comfort zones lately. Lucky for the griffin...and unlucky for us...she was too powerful to be subdued by Patrice's magic.

The amulet's energy was the strongest. The mix of Hecate's high and Lucifer's low vibrations registered in my being, and I scooted down the griffin's back, following the magical pull and searching for a pouch in her skin where she might have hidden it. She was already an eagle and lion combo. Why not kangaroo too?

I kept moving down, running my hands over her fur until...

Oh no.

I moved up to her neck, straddling her back and leaning toward her ear. "I know the guys said you don't understand words any more than a house cat does, but I think they're wrong. I think you understand me, don't you?"

Her purring intensified.

"We want to send you back home so you can raise your babies in peace, but we need your help first." I dug my hands into her feathers, gently gripping them. "I promise no one on the ground will hurt you. Will you please take us down?"

She let out a noise that sounded half-chirp, half-meow, but the communication I received wasn't audible. I couldn't tell you if she put the words into my mind or if I simply felt what she wanted to say, but her message was clear. She just wanted to go home.

"We'll get you home. I promise." I focused on the strange connection we shared. Could all griffins communicate this way, or was it the amulet's doing? At the moment, it didn't matter. "Please take us to the ground so I can tell my team what's happening."

I felt her compliance a moment before she leaped from the branches. I squealed, tightening my grip on her feathers as she flapped her wings. She circled above the trees, and the chilly autumn air whipped my hair back, stinging my cheeks as we soared.

She swooped toward the clearing at a speed that would surely turn into a crash landing, and I forced myself to keep my eyes open. I was riding an effing griffin! Talk about your once-in-a-lifetime experiences.

We didn't crash., thankfully. Instead, she landed softly in the grass and lowered her front end so I could slide off.

"Put your weapons away," I said. "She isn't going to hurt anyone."

Shade and Miles hesitated, their expressions wary, but they sheathed their knives. "How did you tame her?" Miles asked.

"She was already tame. I only comforted her." I glanced at Mayhem. "And she does understand words."

"Amazing." The look of awe in his eyes made my stomach flutter.

"Did you retrieve the amulet?" Chaos asked.

"About that..." I ran my hand down her silky shoulder. "She swallowed it."

CHAPTER 18
MAYHEM

I couldn't tear my gaze away from my witch. Not only had she tamed a creature from Hell, but she had discovered a way to communicate with it that no one had found before. Ember was the strongest, most capable woman I had ever met, and I was in awe of her abilities. Of everything about her.

And she had almost become mine for all eternity.

By opening the rift to Hell, my connection to her had amplified one-hundred-fold. I could no longer tell where my soul ended and hers began. Nor could she, it seemed.

She had tried to cross over, to take me with her. Why had I stopped her? We could have been done with this quest. All the turmoil and strife we had endured could have ended if I'd simply let her step through the rift.

But the feral look in her eyes, the way she'd behaved... I couldn't tell how much of that was Ember versus an amplified version of my own desires. She wasn't completely herself in that moment, and that was why I stopped her.

Had I done the right thing by removing my mark? I wasn't yet sure, but it was the only way I could think to end her hysterics.

I missed the connection the second we severed it. My love for her remained intact. We didn't need a sigil to recognize that we belonged together, but the magical bond we had shared was no more. I was free to do as I pleased, no longer bound to do her bidding. But the emptiness I felt without it made everything clear.

I would choose to serve her for a million eternities before I would endure a single day without her.

"All she wants is to go home. She didn't mean to come here." Ember stood there, resting a hand on the griffin's shoulder as if they were the best of friends. "As soon as the amulet passes through you, the guys will open another rift and send you home."

"Fabulous," Ash said. "The fate of the world lies in the timing of a griffin's bowel movements."

"All we can do is wait for her to pass it." Ember shrugged. "Let's hope she has to poop before she lays her eggs. I'd hate to shove them through a rift not knowing where they'll end up."

"The demons can carry them through when they go home," Patrice said, the tone of her voice indicating the moment couldn't come quickly enough for her liking.

I narrowed my eyes, unable to stop the growl rumbling in my chest. "We are already home."

"That's a sensitive subject." Shade laughed humorlessly. "I've learned not to bring it up."

"I have ipecac syrup." She held up a brown bottle, ignoring the warning. "If you can convince her to drink it, she'll throw up."

"It's already in her intestines." Ember glided her hand down the griffin's side. "The only way it's coming out is through the back door."

The griffin let out a pained groan and lay on her side, the eggs shifting inside her visible beneath her fur. As I stood there in awe of both the creature and my witch, my skin turned to gooseflesh. Vibrations from across the veil registered in my psyche, and I snapped my head toward Chaos, who nodded, confirming my suspicion.

"We must find a safe place to hide her," I said. "The veil is too thin after what we did here. Ember, can you speak to her? Let her know she isn't safe in this location."

My witch kneeled by the beast's head and rested a hand on her feathers. "Can you still move? It's not safe here."

The griffin rolled to her stomach, lying in a sphinx position and watching Ember intently. She let out a quiet squawk and dipped her head as if agreeing.

"She can move." Ember rose to her feet. "She's not in labor yet, but she thinks she will be soon."

"Is she speaking in your mind? Do you hear her voice?" I asked.

"Not really. It's more like I just know." She rolled a length of rope around her arm and handed it to her sister.

"That's an empathic ability," Ash said. "I had no idea you could do that."

"Neither did I." She shrugged. "Go figure, right?"

The goosebumps on my arms turned to pinpricks. "Where can we take her? I can feel the creatures on the other side trying to break through. We must leave this area now."

Ember crossed her arms before tapping a finger to her lips. "We can hide her in the mausoleum where we took out the ghouls. It's big enough for her to lie down, and it's quiet there."

"That's on the other side of Salem," Miles said. "How will we get her there without anyone noticing? She won't fit in the van."

"She'll have to fly," Ember said. "I'll go with her and show her the way. Shade, can you fill the dagger with a shadow so we can stay hidden?"

"I can do that." He held the artifact in his hand and closed his eyes.

"Good. I'll ride her to the mausoleum. The rest of you take the van and meet us there." She tossed the keys to Ash. "Stop by the house and pick up some blankets and whatever we have to feed her. Once we get her settled, Mayhem and I will stay with her until she does the deed."

I smiled as Ember laid out the plan, imagining her commanding a battalion rather than a small coven of witches. She could be a great warrior in the Underworld.

"What will we do after that?" Patrice asked. "I think I should stay with her too. She might need a healer if she gives birth."

"No," Ember said. "I need you to go home and whip up as many salves and healing potions as you can. Come midnight, all Hell is going to break loose."

"Hopefully not *all* of Hell," Ash said.

Ember continued giving orders. "Miles, see if you can get with Wendy. Find out what Adrian is planning. We haven't seen the last of him. Shade and Ash, scry and see if you can find Ignacus and his minions. They're planning something."

"On it." Shade gave a mock salute and handed her the enchanted dagger.

As the witches gathered their things, I stepped

toward Ember and lowered my voice. "I would prefer not to leave your side. Can she carry us both?"

She turned her arm over and gazed at the empty patch of skin where my mark once lay.

"I had no choice." I rested my hand on the small of her back.

She ignored my plea. "Can you carry this big oaf, or is he too heavy?"

She paused, awaiting the griffin's reply. "That makes sense. She said the amulet she accidentally swallowed has made her stronger. She can carry us both."

The others left the clearing, heading for their vehicles, and Ember hoisted herself onto the griffin's back. I joined her, wrapping my arms around her waist, the physical contact filling the void that removing my mark had left behind.

The griffin flapped her wings and rose from the ground to the tops of the trees effortlessly. Ember pointed her in the right direction, and she took off, flying through the late morning sky.

The autumn wind stung my eyes, but I didn't dare close them. The city below resembled a toy replica, appearing gray, unpainted through the shadow hiding us. In all my millennia of existence, I had never considered riding a griffin. Of course, without my witch's newly found ability, capturing one would have caused the beast unnecessary trauma.

Back then, however, I wouldn't have considered the griffin's feelings. The time I had spent here with Ember had changed me in ways I never could have imagined. I held her tighter, resting my chin on her shoulder.

"It's an amazing feeling, isn't it?" she asked.

"Indeed it is."

We arrived at the cemetery in mere minutes, and though I wanted to ask for a longer ride, now was not the time. Most likely, the time for such leisure would never come, but I couldn't think about that.

The griffin touched down outside the mausoleum, and we dismounted. The trees and gravestones in the cemetery appeared charred, the ground covered in fresh dirt that hadn't yet settled.

"You did more than fight ghouls here," I said.

"Whatever gave you that idea?" She held up her hand. "Stay with her while I make sure it's empty."

I did as she asked, waiting outside the structure and doing my best not to scare away the majestic beast beside me. "I will not hurt you. I swear my intention in calling you was to send you home safely."

I quieted, hoping to hear or feel the griffin's response like Ember could. I received no reply.

"It's clear." Ember strode toward us. "Come inside and rest. Our friends are bringing you some food and blankets."

She gestured with her hand, and the griffin

followed her into the chamber. I entered behind the beast and pulled the metal door closed. Ember leaned against a wall as the griffin turned two circles and settled onto her haunches.

"When Ash gets here, we'll set up a ward and cloak her." My witch rubbed her forearm, and my heart wrenched.

I should have felt her touch. My entire body, my soul, should have felt her caress. "Can you reapply my mark?"

She inhaled a shaky breath. "Why did you do it? Why take it away?"

"We both did it. I could not have removed it without your consent."

"I wouldn't have..." She fisted her hands and crossed her arms, pressing her lips into a thin line. "I wasn't myself."

"No, you were not." I tried to hold her gaze, but she wouldn't look at me. The fact that she was not herself was the precise reason I'd convinced her to remove it, but it didn't matter. The deed had been done—by both of us—and now we must face the consequences of my too-quick thinking.

"I wasn't in a state to consent," she said.

"You were an active participant. You severed our connection as I did. It was the only way to stop your hysterics. I couldn't hold open the veil, keep the demons on the other side from crossing over, and call to the griffin while stopping you from dragging me through. Even an immortal prince has his limitations."

She laughed incredulously. "So it's my fault. Is that what you're saying?"

"No, Ember." I strode toward her. "No one is to blame. We did what had to be done."

I took her cheek in my hand, gently guiding her gaze to mine. "It has not changed my feelings for you. We are still soulmates, with or without the mark. Do you not agree?"

She took a deep breath and nuzzled against my palm, her posture finally relaxing. "I agree. I don't like it, but I agree."

She held my hand, pulling it away from her face. "But I wasn't hysterical. I thought we taught you not to use that word in reference to women with emotions."

"You were not yourself." I brushed the hair from her forehead and pressed my lips against it. "Your hysterics came from me."

"How so?" She laced her fingers through mine.

"You were channeling my desires. You could be mine for eternity in the Underworld. I've considered grabbing you and crossing over many times since I came into this realm."

"Why haven't you done it?"

"I could never do anything against your wishes."

"You can now that the sigil is gone." She released

my hand to run her finger over the empty spot on her forearm. "You're a free demon."

I gently grasped her shoulders. "The sigil did not bind me to you in that way. Love did. Love does. I don't need a magical connection to tell me what my soul already knows. I belong to you now and for the rest of eternity."

The griffin huffed and laid her head on her paws.

Ember laughed. "She thinks you're too dramatic."

I tilted my head, pinning her with my gaze. "What do you think?"

She held eye contact, letting seconds pass before she spoke. "I belong to you too, and I don't think the desire I felt to drag you through the rift came entirely from you. Checking out of this reality and starting something new sounds amazing right now."

Resting her hands against my chest, rose onto her toes and kissed me. "But thank you for keeping me grounded. I would have regretted it the second the rift closed behind us."

"My only desire is to make you happy."

She ran her fingers along my jaw, stroking my cheek with her thumb. "I know I don't show it, but you're doing a damn good job."

The griffin grunted and closed her eyes, making Ember smile. "I wish we could keep her."

I shook my head. "She would lose herself. Wild beasts aren't meant to be kept."

Ember looked at me, her eyes searching mine, and I prayed to Lucifer she would find everything she was looking for.

Her lips twitched, tugging into a sad smile. "I know you're not."

CHAPTER 19
EMBER

"I wasn't talking about myself," Mayhem said.

"I know." I pushed from the wall and paced toward the door, tugging my buzzing phone from my pocket on the way. "It's Ash. They're five minutes out."

And thank the goddess for that. I couldn't handle any more sad talk with the demon of my dreams. I sucked at goodbyes, and the finality of ours was ominous. No need to stretch it out from now until the bitter end.

I pulled the door inward and peeked into the cemetery. Everything appeared in full color, meaning the shadow magic I'd borrowed from Shade had fizzled out. We were exposed to the eyes of anyone who might try to venture inside, just as we were exposed to the senses of Ignacus, Adrian, and anyone else who tried to scry for the amulet or the griffin.

Not exactly the safety we'd offered the poor momma.

The minutes inched closer to midnight, to the start of All Hallow's Eve. Normally, my coven would light a bonfire and gather beneath the moon for our annual ritual. We'd give our thanks to the goddess while working in shifts to keep the veil intact until November first was halfway through, when the veil began its return to its normal strength.

We'd managed it well for decades. Hell, probably even centuries. Now, I couldn't begin to fathom what tomorrow would look like. We'd sent way too many powerful beasties back and forth across the veil recently for it to stay intact.

"Are you sure this is a good idea?" A teen girl's voice drew my attention to the left, and I peeked further out the door. She wore a black sweater with a purple witch's hat, which she could have bought anywhere in the city. Everyone sold them, especially this time of year.

"Yeah, it'll be fine." A guy around eighteen walked beside her, a toy store Ouija board tucked under his arm. "I mean it would be better if we waited until dark."

"No!" She tumbled, catching herself on a gravestone before jerking her hand away and wiping her palm on her jeans. "I don't want to be here at night. It's scary enough now."

The back of my throat heated with my annoyed sigh. This cemetery? Seriously? There were plenty of old graveyards where famous…or infamous…Salem residents were buried. This wasn't one of them.

"What's wrong?" Mayhem asked.

"I was hoping not to rack up any more mundane casualties." I rolled my eyes as the guy set the board on a gravestone and rested the plastic planchette in the center.

"Would you like me to get rid of them?" He stood beside me, touching the small of my back.

"I'll handle it." It had been a while since I'd gotten the chance to put the fear of witchcraft into an idiot.

"Put your fingers on the planchette." The guy grabbed the girl's wrist and forced her hand onto the board.

"I don't want to." She tried to pull away, but he held her tightly. "This doesn't feel right, James."

I tugged a dagger from my thigh holster, set the tip ablaze, and strolled toward them. "Oh, James. You really should let the dead rest in peace. You never know what you might stir up."

I touched my index finger to the flat side of my blade, letting the flames lick across my skin.

"It was his idea." The girl scrambled to her feet. "He said we could summon my dog."

James rose and gestured at my dagger. "Where'd you get that? How does it work?"

"It's been in my family for generations." Yes, that was a lie, but I wasn't about to tell him I bought it online. Where was the fun in that?

"Let me see it." He had the audacity to reach toward me, his body language saying he fully expected me to hand it over. If I hadn't been fired, I'd have no doubt I'd see this asshat at Spellbound Axe, getting drunk with his buddies and bouncing blades off the targets.

"Sure." I shot a tiny flame at his hand, singeing his sleeve.

"Ow! What the hell?" He sauntered closer. "Who are you?"

"She'll be your worst nightmare if you take another step forward," Mayhem said from behind me.

James's eyes widened, and he cut his gaze between me, my demon, and the girl. "I don't know what kind of kinky shit you have going on here, but we're gonna walk away and pretend we never saw it."

"That's the first intelligent thing I've heard you say." I extinguished the flames and returned my dagger to its holster.

The girl whimpered, and the guy grabbed her

hand. "Come on, Jill. We'll find somewhere else to summon Princess Fancy Pants."

He dragged her away, and I turned around to find Mayhem looming behind me, his horns and talons extended. No wonder the guy changed his tune mid-measure.

I clicked my tongue. "Put those away. You're lucky it's almost Halloween and they can pass as a costume."

"What did you do to them?" Ash laughed as she approached from the direction the kids had run. She carried a bundle of towels in her arms, and her satchel bounced against her hip with her strides.

Chaos carried a stack of blankets, and several grocery bags dangled from his fingers. "He mumbled something about twisted cemetery orgies as they ran for their car."

I waved off their concern. "He was planning to use Princess Fancy Pants to get into *her* pants."

Ash's brow scrunched. "I'm not even going to ask. How's the griffin?"

"She's resting." I took the towels from her and carried them into the mausoleum. "Where are the guys?"

"Scrying. Miles got ahold of Wendy, but she wasn't much help." Ash took her bag off her shoulder and pulled out four railroad spikes. "Adrian has locked himself in his office and isn't communicating with his team, so she has no idea what he's planning. She's waiting outside his door, though, just for Miles."

"Clueless," I said.

"Yep." She rubbed oil on the spikes.

Chaos stepped into the mausoleum with Mayhem behind him. "Where should I put these?"

"Lay them next to her for now. When she gets up, I'll make her a bed." I took the mallet Ash offered and followed her outside.

She handed me a spike, and I hammered it into the ground at the eastern corner. I did the same at the southern before we made our way around the back of the building.

"How does it feel?" She gestured to my sigil-less arm and then pressed her hand to her chest. "Does it hurt?"

"Only when I think about it." I hammered the third spike into the ground, focusing on the vibration shim-mying up my arm every time it made impact.

She handed me the final spike. "Do you still…?"

I forced my jaw to unclench. "Love him desper-ately? Yeah."

Whack, whack, whack. I drove in the last piece and rose to my feet. "Let's get this ward cast before Adrian emerges from his hidey hole."

She took my hand, and we recited the incanta-tions. "Protect this space from malice and harm. If our ward is broken, we will be warned. Hide our auras from all who seek. Our intention is set with the words we speak. As we will it, so mote it be."

My head spun with the amount of vim we put into it, but we'd recover. We always did, even before we could channel demon magic on the regular. We'd be fine without them... Wouldn't we?

Stop it, Em. Just. Stop.

"That should do it," Ash said. "It would take every witch in Adrian's coven working together to see through that shroud."

"And everyone knows dark witches don't play well with others." I gave her the mallet, and we walked into the building to find Mayhem hand-feeding the griffin raw chicken breasts.

I curled my lip. "You're feeding bird meat to a bird."

"She is not a bird," Mayhem said. "But even if she were, what do you think eagles eat if not other, smaller fowl?"

"I see your point." I sat cross-legged in front of the grocery bags. "Did you bring anything for us? I'm starving."

"Here." Ash opened a bag and pulled out a container of chicken salad and a loaf of bread.

"I guess your credit card isn't maxed out yet?" I used a plastic spoon to scoop out the mixture and spread it on the bread.

"No, it is." She glanced at Chaos. "But we have to eat."

I didn't have the energy to protest, so I handed Mayhem a sandwich before making myself one.

"I also brought this for her." Ash pulled out a jug of water, a plastic bowl, and a white plastic bag with purple lettering.

"Epsom salt?" I poured the water into the bowl.

"It's a natural laxative." She added the salt and stirred it with the plastic spoon. "To help speed things along."

I set the bowl in front of the griffin, and she dipped her beak into it before tilting her head back to swallow.

Ash's phone pinged, and she swiped open the screen. "It's Miles. Still no sign of Ignacus or his soldiers, but the team reported a lesser fae swarm in the Common. He and Shade helped them take care of it."

I chugged a bottle of water. "Tell them to start the All Hallow's Eve ritual now. Every member of the coven is required to participate. No one gets a pass this year. If Hecate is the only person holding the veil together right now, we need to give her all the help we can."

"Only the High Priestess can begin the ceremony," Ash said. "The wood has to be lit by witch fire."

"Which means any Holland can do it, not just the

High Priestess. It starts with the founding family and spreads outward. You'll have to light it." I picked up her satchel and shoved it toward her. "Take Chaos and begin the ritual. I'm staying with the griffin until she poops."

Ash gave me her signature look. The one that said everything on her mind, no words required. The ritual always started with the High Priestess. All the ones we had records of anyway. Changing tradition could be risky. I knew that, but I doubted she could name one thing we'd done in the past month that wasn't.

She also didn't like splitting up the team. Neither did I.

"You can call them to do it here if you want, but I'm not leaving her." I took the empty bowl o' laxative and shoved it into a grocery bag.

Ash's jaw ticked, her expression a silent acquiescence. "One fire in this cemetery was more than enough, thanks. I'll get it started in the usual clearing."

"Good. Leave Patrice in charge of the first shift and then go home to set up Discord's summoning circle. With any luck, we'll complete the amulet and join you well before midnight."

The griffin stood and turned a circle, pawing at the blankets and arranging them beneath her before she settled and closed her eyes.

"At this rate, I'll have to poop before she does." Ash

swiped open her phone, her brow furrowing as she typed and scrolled.

"What are you looking for?" Chaos asked as he gathered the bags they'd brought.

"When I was little, I swallowed a tiny lion figurine. I remember being in a lot of pain because it wouldn't pass. Dad wanted to take me to the hospital, but Mom tried Joan, our old healer, first. She cast a spell that drew it out. It was... Oh, I think this might be it."

She rummaged through her bag and held up an herb jar triumphantly. "I have everything here." She dropped to her knees and started mixing.

I took her phone and studied the recipe. "This sounds...forceful."

"It is, and it will make a mess. We'll have to take her outside." She sprinkled amaranth into a copper bowl and added a dash of star anise and marjoram. "We'll focus on drawing the amulet out, but pretty much everything in the way will come out too."

"Will your ward protect her outside?" Mayhem asked.

"We only protected the building." Ash scooped a drop of wildflower honey from a small jar but hesitated to drop it into the bowl. "Crappity crap, we should have made the ward bigger. It's not a quick and easy spell."

"So, we'll point her butt out the door." I shrugged and set the phone by the bowl. "Guys, you can stand outside and retrieve the amulet from wherever it lands."

Mayhem clapped Chaos on the shoulder. "Come, brother. We've been banished to the path of the poo."

"You don't have to stand exactly in her line of fire." I rolled my eyes as they exited the building and took up their posts on either side of the door.

"Hey, sweet girl." I stroked the griffin's feathers, rousing her from sleep. "I know you're tired, but we need you to move one more time. This won't be pleasant, but it'll get you home faster."

She grumbled, but she got up and let us arrange the blankets for her by the door. When she plopped down, her tail hung outside. Mayhem lifted it and tucked it inside the building. Ash added two drops of honey to the potion, making it pop and sizzle before she handed the bowl to me.

"Let's get Operation Beastie Bowels underway. We need you to drink this." I set the bowl in front of the griffin, and she sniffed it before turning her head away.

"Please." I laid a hand on her shoulder. "It will help you feel better."

She eyed me for a moment, and my stomach clenched. She'd been compliant so far, but her agitation was growing, even with me. All she wanted to do was sleep. I knew the feeling.

Finally, she huffed and drank the potion. Ash took

my hand and rested her other on the griffin's belly. I did the same, and we recited the incantation.

The beastie's abdomen rumbled, her intestines squelching and groaning. When they quieted, we recited the incantation again.

"Focus on the amulet," Ash said. "Use your intent to draw it down."

I felt the stone inside her and moved my hand over it, brushing her fur downward toward her backside. The griffin moaned, her insides cramping. She made sure I knew what it felt like. I had never experienced labor pains, but I imagined it was similar.

Slowly, steadily, the amulet made its way through her intestines. Every time her body stilled, we recited the incantation again, causing the poor beastie more pain, but getting the amulet closer and closer to the exit.

Her stomach bubbled. A puff of noxious gas shot out her backside, the stench so strong it could have melted the eyebrows off anyone in its path. We said the spell one more time. She rumbled and groaned.

"Get ready." Ash massaged her belly.

"Thar she blows!" I covered my mouth and pinched my nose as our spell peaked, showing us its full effect.

And I mean its *full* effect. Capital F-U-L-L.

The griffin's butt cannon did its thing, shooting out everything she'd consumed in goddess knew how long. I expected the forceful blast to travel at least five yards out, taking the amulet with it.

But the prize for the absolute worst timing in the history of showing up at places you weren't supposed to be went to Adrian and his crew.

Three witches stood a few feet outside the door, covered from head to toe in wet, steaming griffin poop.

CHAPTER 20
EMBER

We all stood there in shock, staring at each other, no one moving at first. Miles's friend Wendy flanked Adrian on his left, and Gray, who had dropped her shadow magic when the shit hit the witch, stood to his right. Her lower lip trembled, and she pressed it against her top, not daring to open her mouth and complain.

I couldn't blame her. She had feces dripping down her face and nothing to wipe it off with. *Gross.*

"How did you find us?" I scanned the ground, looking for the amulet. It must have blasted past our adversaries.

Adrian stared at the doorway, narrowing his eyes like he couldn't see where the voice was coming from.

Oh, right. Our ward.

Mayhem stepped away from the building, and

Adrian's gaze snapped to him, his expression livid. Chaos tossed a roll of paper towels at Gray's feet, and she picked it up, unrolling several and cleaning herself before passing it to Adrian.

With her face semi-clear, she took a chance and opened her mouth. "Please tell me this isn't..."

"Explosive diarrhea straight from the bowels of Hell?" I crossed my arms. "Yeah, you deserve it for summoning her to do your dirty work." They were lucky the poor beastie hadn't become an egg cannon too.

"We didn't summon her," Gray said, cutting her eyes to her High Priest. "Did we?"

"Hand her over." Adrian cleaned himself up and dropped the rest of the roll onto the ground, not bothering to pass it to Wendy. Typical. She bent to pick it up.

I laughed, still scanning the ground for the amulet. I couldn't see it, so I stepped around the beastie and stood just outside the doorway. "I don't take orders like your minions."

The griffin let out a relieved moan behind me, curling up to rest, and Ash joined me on the front steps. "Do you see it?" she whispered.

I gave my head a tiny shake. "Did Ignacus tell you where we were? I know you aren't strong enough to see through our ward on your own."

"We have our ways of finding information." Adrian

jerked the roll of towels from Wendy's hand and wiped his face again before dragging the cloth down his neck. "Your van is parked outside, idiot. Turn over the griffin. The amulet belongs to me."

Wendy blew her nose and gagged. "This is not what I signed up for." She covered her mouth and dry heaved. "Where's Miles?"

I cocked my head. Did she seriously volunteer to be Adrian's henchwoman just so she could see a guy who'd used her...multiple times? Goddess, bless her heart.

Ash crept away from the mausoleum, giving our foul-smelling foes a wide berth as she scanned the ground. It had to be out here somewhere, but the clouds covering the moon made it nearly impossible to decipher the shapes on the ground. Shadows, clumps of earth, and dead leaves littered the cemetery, and even if we had enough moonlight to make the stone glint, it was covered in dirt-colored poo.

"You can't have the amulet or the griffin." I crept away from the door, trusting the ward to keep the bad guys out. "It's four elementals against you and..." I gestured at Gray and Wendy. "You didn't call in much of a calvary."

Ash lit a fireball in her hand, and Chaos and Mayhem followed her lead, illuminating the cemetery. I unsheathed my trusty sword and sent flames licking up the enchanted silver blade, adding to the brightness, but honestly? I preferred the dark over what I saw.

Twenty-something witches, dressed in black from head to toe, emerged from the shadows. They stepped around gravestones and came out from the cover of trees as if appearing from nothing.

They surrounded us, some of their faces familiar, some I'd never seen before. Many had the Boston Society of Magic emblem embroidered in silver thread on their sleeves. Others had nothing showing affiliation to the dark coven, and of those, a few wore ski masks, hiding their identities.

"Did you hire mercenaries?" I adjusted my grip on the sword, scanning the ground again before meeting his gaze. "Seriously?"

"I'll do whatever it takes to obtain the amulet." He circled his finger, creating the beginnings of a tornado at my feet. "Did you know it was forged in Hell? Anything created in Hell belongs with a dark witch."

He raised his hand, palm toward me, and I had no doubt he was about to give his team the signal to attack.

I cut my gaze to Ash and closed my eyes for a long blink, hoping to Hecate she would understand the message. We weren't going to find the amulet with our eyes. Not in these conditions.

She nodded and inhaled, and we both whispered the same spell, "Confess, expose my magic sleuth. I call on you to reveal your truth."

I shouldn't have been able to tap into her magic from this distance. Normally, we had to hold hands to cast spells together, but golden sparkles appeared in my peripheral vision anyway. I slowly turned my head to the place they gathered on the ground, two yards from Wendy's feet.

Adrian clenched his raised hand into a fist. The witches attacked.

Mayhem turned his arm into a blow torch and blasted hellfire at our adversaries. I dove toward Wendy, extinguishing my blade and swinging the flat side into her stomach like a baseball bat. She doubled over. Then she fell to her knees. Her hands hit the ground, and she gasped.

"Adrian? Is this it?" She lifted the amulet caked in butt dumplings and turned on her knees toward him.

"Nope." I kicked her hand, and the stone flew across the cemetery before whacking into an ancient gravestone with such force, the monument cracked. Good thing the amulet didn't.

"Ash!" I shouted, and she scrambled toward it.

A blade pierced my shoulder, and I spun, lighting my sword. Instinct nearly made me cut the culpable witch in two. I was used to fighting beasties, not people. Lucky for the guy who'd stabbed me, I remembered what he was and only nicked his arm, setting his embroidered sleeve ablaze.

His shirt must've been one hundred percent cotton, because the fire spread like...well, like wildfire...engulfing his entire abdomen. He screamed, frantically turning this way and that, fanning the flames.

"Did no one teach you to stop, drop, and roll when you were a kid?" I called my fire back, leaving him shirtless and burned, as I yanked his knife from my shoulder. That would require stitches. Where was Patrice when we needed her?

Oh, right. I'd sent her home.

The man gritted his teeth and pulled two more blades from their sheathes. He lunged for me.

I stepped out of his way. "Do you want me to make you pantsless too? I'd rather not singe your naughty bits."

His eye twitched, but he backed away. Smart move.

All around me, shouted spells, clashing weapons, and crackling fire created a cacophony of *we don't have time for this shit.*

Ash reached for the amulet, but someone hit her with an asphyxiation spell. She clutched her throat and fell to her knees, unable to drag in a breath.

I scanned the crowd, searching for the witch responsible. "Chaos, red ponytail."

The witch stood still, her hands raised toward my suffocating sister. This one, I would have gladly sliced in half, but Chaos beat me to it. He snapped her neck as if her bones were made of toothpicks. Her body smacked the earth, and Ash gasped.

Another of Adrian's minions grabbed the amulet. Based on the person's size and curves, she had to be a woman, but the ski mask hid all but her eyes and mouth. She smiled and wiped the poo off the pendant before moving to drop it into her pocket.

"That's mine. You will give it to me," Chaos said, holding Ash's hand and channeling their mind-control magic. If only they could control everyone here and send them on their way.

The woman froze, her hand fisting around the chain. "I think this is yours."

"No!" Adrian sent his tornado toward her, whisking it from her hand and sending it spiraling upward.

"A rift is forming," Mayhem said as he lit a ring of hellfire around us, blocking at least fifteen witches. "Ignacus."

I threw a hand in the air. "For goddess's sake, Adrian. Do you ever fight your own fights?"

"I didn't call him." He reached upward, and his tornado obeyed, spiraling above us. When he fisted his hand, it dissipated, the amulet dropping from the sky.

He caught it and cradled it in his hands, closing his eyes and absorbing its power.

When he opened them, a blast of wind shot out around him, knocking me off my feet and extinguishing our ring of fire. The rift opened fully, and five fae soldiers darted through.

The biggest bug man lunged straight for a mercenary, ripping out his liver with one hand, his heart with the other. He kneeled in front of the rift, lowering his head and holding the organs up in offering.

Ignacus stepped through, one spindly leg at a time, and the other fae bowed at his entrance. His mandibles made a clicking sound, his dinner squelching with each bite as he consumed first the liver, and then the heart.

His soldiers joined the fray, no doubt ready to eat every liver and heart still beating in the cemetery. The good thing about his arrival? Adrian's witches were now busy fighting for their lives instead of trying to take ours.

The bad? Ash and I were the strongest, most potent witches they could consume. It was best they didn't find that out.

Still clutching the amulet, Adrian sent a blast of wind toward Ignacus, his newly multiplied magic allowing him to scoop up the fae prince and toss him against the mausoleum wall as if he were a ragdoll.

Our ward on the building sent a shockwave

through his exoskeleton, his body convulsing as he landed face-first in the dirt. He jerked his head up and flapped his wings, sending dirt flying everywhere as he shook himself off.

Ignacus made a high-pitched chittering sound, and his soldiers dropped the witches they were tearing apart to descend upon us.

Ash shot a stream of flames at one. Chaos hurled a ball of hellfire at another. It bounced off the soldier's chest and set an already-scorched tree ablaze.

"Let the record state I am not responsible for the cemetery fire this time." Ash called her flames back and shot out an even hotter stream.

Adrian's idiotic team followed the fae, breaking blades against their armor and wasting their vim on spells that could be fanned away with a flap of their wings.

I grabbed Mayhem's hand. "Make the violence stop."

"You no longer bear my mark. The connection is..."

"It's still there." I squeezed his hand tighter. "Tell me you don't feel it."

"I do, but the magic is not as strong." He threw a fireball at Adrian, who retaliated with a gust of wind, averting the hellfire's path.

"Then make it stronger." I focused, not on the tattoo once occupying my forearm, but on the real connection I had with my demon. Magical ink hadn't forged our bond. Fate had, and I didn't need a sigil to link to my soulmate.

I opened and sent my magic into him, picturing my light filling the darkness inside him. He inhaled deeply and opened to me, allowing our vim to pass freely back and forth, to mix and meld and become one force. Two parts of a whole coming together, complete at last.

My pulse raced as he sent it outward. Pinpricks danced across my skin, my blood seeming to fizz as he calmed the entire calamity, making everyone freeze and scratch their heads, wondering what they were fighting for.

"Go home," Chaos said to Gray. He held Ash's hand, their intention apparently to make each witch leave, one by one, as long as we held them in peace.

"Leave this place," he said to Wendy.

She held up her hands in surrender and backed away. "I just wanted to see Miles. Is he still alive? He hasn't sounded like himself in his texts."

"He's fine," Ash said.

"Please hand over the amulet." Ignacus held a gangly hand toward Adrian. "I do not wish to fight."

Sweat beaded on my forehead even though it was only fifty degrees out. I could admit the tattoo had made it a helluva lot easier to pull this off, but here we were, pulling it off anyway.

Adrian scoffed. Then he laughed. "Did you think

your mind magic would work on me? I'm unstoppable now." He created a wind funnel around a soldier, lifting the beastie from the ground and cracking the exoskeleton as he drew the air from the fae's lungs.

I slipped a dagger from my thigh holster. As much as I would have loved to watch him implode every fae here, we needed that amulet. Now.

I lifted my arm, ready to throw the blade, when the griffin's pained bellow registered in my psyche. "She's about to lay her eggs. You have to open a rift and send her home."

"I am a bit busy, as are you."

I strained, goosebumps rising on my skin as I flushed first hot and then cold. "I can't do this much longer anyway. Go help her."

"If I release them, you will have to fight."

"Fighting is what I do best."

He looked at me, his eyes searching mine before he nodded once and tugged from my grasp. I sucked in a breath as he turned and strode into the mausoleum. I hurled my dagger at Adrian. The blade sank into his shoulder.

He yanked it out, losing his grip on the semi-crushed fae. The fly man thudded on the ground, and a witch in a ski mask jabbed a knife beneath an armored plate, piercing his heart. She shot to her feet, brushing her hands on her pants before scurrying behind the mausoleum. If she was smart, she'd keep going and not come back.

"It's done." Chaos dropped Ash's hand and stepped away from her. "He has opened the rift."

Good. At least the poor griffin, who'd wanted no part in any of this, could go home and raise her babies in peace.

"I feel another forming," Chaos said. "We must end this before more creatures descend upon us. They're attracted to our power."

"Let them come." Adrian draped the amulet around his neck. "No one can stop me."

The four remaining soldiers encircled Adrian, but he created a wind tunnel around himself, blocking them. What was left of his witch posse charged us, but Ash and I created another fire circle, encompassing us and the fae.

The soldiers took to the air, divebombing Adrian, but he pushed them away with gusts of wind, his power growing stronger by the minute, his laugh more maniacal, his eyes more crazed. His funnel tightened, lifting him from the ground before spreading outward, the spiral creating a suction that pulled in leaves, dirt, and broken branches, creating a bramble around him.

We had to stop him before he sucked the entire cemetery—and everyone in it—into his storm.

"How is he so strong so fast?" I shielded my eyes

and inched toward him while Chaos kept the fire circle blazing.

"It's the biggest piece of the amulet." Ash's hair whipped back as she leaned into the wind, pushing toward Adrian. His funnel shifted, the wind changing direction in an instant. Ash's hair flew into her face, her already forward momentum adding to the drag and making her stumble to her hands and knees.

"He's also an elemental," Chaos said. "The more powerful the being, the more efficiently the amulet amplifies their power."

"And the crazier it makes them." I leaned back, digging my boots into the dirt as Adrian's funnel tried to pull me into it.

My chest squeezed, the griffin's goodbye echoing in my soul. I tried to send her a peaceful sentiment in return, but my foot snagged on an exposed root. I careened forward, landing on my stomach a yard from the bottom of the tornado.

Chaos hauled Ash up by the arm. A fae soldier dive-bombed them. I army-crawled toward the wind funnel, scrambling to my feet beneath it and latching onto Adrian's ankle.

Holy Hecate on a unicycle.

Even through his clothes, the power from the amulet surged through my body, setting my nerves ablaze. He kicked, smacking the side of my head before I grabbed his other leg and hauled myself up. I clutched one hip, then the other, and tried not to think about the fact that my face pressed into his crotch.

And that his clothes were still coated in beastie biscuits and gravy.

My stomach lurched. Thankfully, my innards ignored the command to spew chicken salad all over the place, and I reached higher, clutching his shoulder with one hand, the amulet with the other.

Talk about your power surges. Damn.

My muscles seized, my hands tightening into unbreakable fists, my inborn fire rising to the surface, setting my skin ablaze. I pried my hand from Adrian's shoulder and let myself fall, the chain snapping off his neck with a jerk of my arm.

We weren't that high. A straight fall to the ground might've bruised me a little, but of course, I hadn't thought my escape through.

I did not fall straight to the ground. In fact, I got caught in the spiraling tornado, and it slung me around like a rotating catapult, flinging me against the trunk of a massive birch. Every ounce of air left my lungs in a whoosh, and my vision tunneled and wavered.

The impact nearly bent me in two. My vertebrae cracked like a glowstick, and if I had hit it at an angle a few degrees different, I had no doubt I'd have been paralyzed.

Instead, I pushed to sitting, my head still swimming, and tried to make my eyes focus. My sister dragged Adrian to the ground. Chaos ripped a pincher from a soldier's mandible. Mayhem stood on the mausoleum steps, his taloned fingers wrapped around another soldier's neck. Witch fire mixed with hellfire blazed all around us.

Something made impact with the side of my head.

My face smacked the earth, filling my mouth with charred dirt. I spit and sat upright, the amulet giving me strength to endure what should have rendered me unconscious.

Ignacus loomed over me, poisonous saliva dripping from his pinchers as he slammed a barbed insect foot into my wrist, pinning me to the ground. He pressed one wiry hand against my stomach and snatched the amulet from my grasp with another.

I tried to pull my wrist free, but the barbs protruding from his foot dug into my flesh. I'd have to take off my entire hand to free myself...*if* he didn't rip out my liver first.

I slid my free hand down my thigh in search of a blade. I could live with only one hand.

Ignacus raised the amulet triumphantly. I could feel the power surging through him, burning my wrist where he'd penetrated it.

He snapped his gaze to me, his expression livid. "Where is the rest of it?"

"I have no idea what you mean." My fingers brushed the pommel of my dagger.

He grunted. Then he growled. He opened his mouth, and the most freakish chittering sound I'd ever heard emanated from his throat. Barbs extended from the tips of his fingers, cutting through my shirt and into my skin.

With the amulet amplifying everything, I felt his energy coil in his shoulder half a nanosecond before he plunged his claws into my stomach.

CHAPTER 21

EMBER

A screech sounded from inside the mausoleum. Ignacus paused, his claws an inch inside my flesh, and jerked his head toward the sound. The griffin barreled toward us.

The piercing pain in my abdomen made everything that happened next foggy, but one second, I was laid out on the ground, a feast for the fae prince, and the next, I lay there alone, the gouges in my abs and wrist bleeding profusely.

I pressed my injured arm to the puncture in my stomach and applied pressure with my free hand.

The griffin took to the sky, the fae prince's head in her beak, his body flailing as it dangled from her grip. She flapped her massive wings, turning herself vertically and clutching Ignacus with all four of her murder mittens.

Then, she jerked his head clean off.

She spit, and the head hit the ground, bouncing once before rolling into the ring of fire. With another ear-piercing screech, she shot to the earth, slamming him down and literally ripping him limb from limb and throwing all the pieces into the fire too.

Only his torso remained, but I wasn't taking any chances. I grabbed the dagger I'd been trying to reach, marched toward our fractured foe, and slammed it beneath a breastplate, piercing his heart.

"Em, the amulet is in the fire," Ash shouted. "Call yours back."

I did as she asked and stroked the griffin's feathers. "Thank you."

She nodded *you're welcome* and turned toward Mayhem.

"She refused to leave until you were safe." He dropped a lifeless soldier onto the ground. "My cousin Havoc is keeping the demons at bay across the rift, but he can't hold them forever."

"Go now." I threw my arms around her neck and hugged her tightly. "Lay your eggs in peace."

I walked with her to the mausoleum and stood outside the doorway, careful not to get too close to the rift, lest I try to pull Mayhem through again. As she lifted a paw to step through, she turned to me, thanking me again.

"Thank *you*." I pressed my palms together, my

chest squeezing as she disappeared into the Underworld. "She said we can call her if we ever need her again."

"A noble beast, indeed." Mayhem waved a hand, sealing the rift he'd created.

I turned toward the cemetery and took in the aftermath. The remaining fae scurried through the rift their prince had created, but without his power, they couldn't seal it. Or maybe they could have, but they preferred to hightail it home and beg the king for forgiveness. Either way, it left the job to Ash and me.

Adrian's coven had long since retreated, leaving him alone with us. Ash picked up the amulet, and he lunged, his eyes still wild with affliction.

Chaos caught him by the throat. "Are you sure I can't kill him?"

Ash blinked, looking at him briefly before returning her attention to the amulet lying in her palm. "Yeah, that's fine. Do whatever."

"Chaos, don't," I shouted as Adrian summoned his witch wind, creating a funnel around himself. "Let him go."

Chaos scoffed. "Ash told me I—"

"Ash isn't herself." Mayhem crept toward her. "Perhaps I should hold onto that."

She clenched her fist around the pendant. "The hell you should."

Chaos released his hold, and Adrian's tornado

whisked him away. Ten minutes in contact with the amulet, and he could already fly. What would it do to my sister?

"Ash, give it to Mayhem." I cautiously walked toward her. "Remember what that one small piece did to Chrys? I won't let that happen to you."

Her nostrils flared, her jaw clenching. "He's been trying to get his hands on this since we summoned him. No. No way."

Her sigil glowed, Chaos sending his calming energy into her. "Allow me to hold it, little witch. I'll keep you, and it, safe."

She tilted her head at her demon. "My powers have been bound my entire life. I deserve a little boost."

"Indeed you do, my love. But not with a fractured piece. It will damage your mind." He held his hand toward her.

"You need to get it," I whispered to Mayhem. "You're the only one I trust."

He moved so quickly, I nearly missed it. I would have if I'd blinked. He shot out an arm, gripping her wrist and yanking the amulet from her grasp before she realized what was happening.

She gasped and stiffened, her lower lip trembling for a moment before her posture slumped. "That was..."

"*Lord of the* Rings intense?" I asked.

"Yeah." She heaved in another breath. "Thanks for taking it."

Mayhem held the chain between two fingers, letting the pendant dangle in front of him. "We should take this home before anyone else tries to intercept it."

"Yeah." She rubbed her palms on her pants. "What about the mess?"

Leave it to my sister to worry about a mess when we had a world to save. Then again, leaving a fae rift open and bodies of overgrown insects littering the ground wasn't a good idea either.

"Guys, gather the fae parts and shove them through the rift. Ash and I will cremate the witches and pick up the griffin's blankets."

Ash applied a salve and bandages to my wounds before we worked together, cleaning up the evidence. My sister and I sealed the rift, and we carried everything to the van. Chaos drove, giving me a chance to recharge in the back seat with Mayhem.

"How are your injuries?" he asked, stroking my hair as I lay in his lap.

"I'll survive. I got a little boost through Adrian and then Ignacus when they had the amulet. Looks like it speeds up healing too."

"It is capable of a great many things." He ran his fingers over my injured wrist. "No pain?"

"Not anymore." I sat upright and rested my chin on his shoulder. "Why haven't you used it?"

He blew a breath through his nose and laughed softly. "Why would I? I have everything I've ever wanted, all I'll ever need, right here with you."

"Me too. Almost." I snuggled against him and closed my eyes. I had everything I never knew I wanted in him too.

My stomach sank as we pulled into the drive behind our building. This was it. Everything we'd been working toward was about to come to fruition, with a few hours to spare. We remained silent as we entered through the back door, a heaviness settling over us as we trudged upstairs to get the rest of the amulet.

Mayhem set the newest piece on the counter, and I lay a massive blue vibrator next to it.

He chuckled. "I see I've changed your opinion on what's needed for a good time."

"You have no idea." I waved my hand over it, disintegrating the shroud and revealing the rest of the stone.

Using Ash's biggest tweezers, I picked it up and touched it to the shard we'd just obtained. It glowed brightly, blindingly. I shielded my eyes against the flashes and sparks, and when it was through, the most powerful magical artifact I had ever encountered... maybe that even existed...lay on our kitchen counter.

I glanced at the clock. "Next steps. We have to start the All Hallow's Eve ritual. Ash, take Chaos and gather the coven in the clearing. Start the fire, and then meet us in your studio. I'll prepare the circle and have every-thing ready for the summoning when you get back."

She eyed the amulet and rested her hand next to it. "It really should be you who starts it. I can stay and set everything up."

"Not a chance." I grabbed the chain and handed it to Mayhem.

She blinked three times rapidly. "Yeah. You're right. They should already be gathering, so give me half an hour."

"Perfect," I said.

We all headed downstairs, Chaos and Ash hanging a left to go outside, Mayhem and I going right to set up what would be our final summoning circle.

He watched as I poured the salt and used chalk to sketch his eldest brother's sigil in the center of the ring. "You drew it perfectly, yet I felt ill watching it happen."

I stood and dusted off my knees. "That's because you're my demon. It felt gross to draw it, honestly. I hope I never have to do it again."

I opened the grimoire we'd used to summon Mayhem. We'd bookmarked both the summoning and the containment spells, but I already had them memo-rized. "Miles and Shade are good to stay at the ritual, right? Since we have the amulet, Discord should be easy to summon."

"Relatively." He grasped my waist and tugged me

toward him. "When our siblings return, things will happen quickly."

"I know." I swallowed the thickness from my throat. "But it has to be done."

He searched my eyes, a sheen forming over his as he held my gaze. "I love you, Ember Holland."

I clasped my hands behind his neck. "And I love you, Mayhem, Prince of Hell."

He kissed my forehead before resting his against it. "I promise to love you every second of every day, with every fiber of my being, for all of eternity."

A sob threatened to roll up from my chest, but I cleared my throat, chasing it away. "Me too."

The insistent sob tried again, and this time, I let it pass my lips. He cupped my face in his hands, the intensity of his gaze rooting me to the spot. I half-expected him to make promises he could never keep. To lie and say he would find a way to return. That everything would be okay.

Part of me wanted him to tell me lies.

But he didn't say a word.

My phone buzzed in my pocket with a call trying to interrupt our moment. I ignored it and leaned against my demon, holding him tightly and resting my head on his shoulder. Three seconds after the call silenced, it started again.

I sighed heavily and looked at the screen. "It's Ash. I better answer."

He held me tighter as I pressed the device to my ear and said, "Hello."

"You must perform the summoning without us." It was Chaos, not Ash, and I did not like his alarming tone.

My heart slammed against my chest as I straightened. "Why? What happened?"

He missed a beat...two...three, making my stomach sink. "It's Ash," he finally said. "She set Shade on fire."

ALSO BY CARRIE PULKINEN

Fire Witches of Salem Series

Chaos and Ash

Commanding Chaos

Claiming Chaos

Mayhem and Ember

Mending Mayhem

Mastering Mayhem

Collection One: Books 1-3

Collection Two: Books 4-6

Crescent City Wolf Pack Series

Werewolves Only

Beneath a Blue Moon

Bound by Blood

A Deal with Death

A Song to Remember

Shifting Fate

Collection One: Books 1-3

Collection Two: Books 4-6

New Orleans Nocturnes Series

License to Bite

Shift Happens

Life's a Witch

Santa Got Run Over by a Vampire

Finders Reapers

Swipe Right to Bite

Batshift Crazy

Collection One: Books 1-3

Collection Two: Books 4-7

Haunted Ever After Series

Love at First Haunt

Second Chance Spirit

Third Time's a Ghost

Love and Ghosts

Love and Omens

Love and Curses

Collection One: Books 1 - 3

Collection Two: Books 4 - 6

Stand Alone Books

Flipping the Bird

Sign Steal Deliver

Azrael

Lilith

The Rest of Forever

Soul Catchers

Bewitching the Vampire

About the Author

Carrie Pulkinen is a paranormal romance author who has always been fascinated with things that go bump in the night. Of course, when you grow up next door to a cemetery, the dead (and the undead) are hard to ignore. Pair that with her passion for writing and her love of a good happily-ever-after, and becoming a paranormal romance author seems like the only logical career choice.

Before she decided to turn her love of the written word into a career, Carrie spent the first part of her professional life as a high school journalism and yearbook teacher. She loves good chocolate and bad puns, and in her free time, she likes to read, drink wine, and travel with her family.

Connect with Carrie online:
CarriePulkinen.com